CHANG

THE YELLOW CHIEF

BY GLEN ROWBERRY

Order this book online at www.trafford.com/09-0120
or email orders@trafford.com

Most Trafford titles are also available at major online book retailers.

Note for Librarians: A cataloguing record for this book is available from Library
and Archives Canada at www.collectionscanada.ca/amicus/index-e.html

Printed in Victoria, BC, Canada.

ISBN: 978-1-4269-0296-3 (soft)
ISBN: 978-1-4269-0300-7 (ebook)

*We at Trafford believe that it is the responsibility of us all, as both individuals
and corporations, to make choices that are environmentally and socially sound.
You, in turn, are supporting this responsible conduct each time you purchase a
Trafford book, or make use of our publishing services. To find out how you are
helping, please visit www.trafford.com/responsiblepublishing.html*

*Our mission is to efficiently provide the world's finest, most comprehensive
book publishing service, enabling every author to experience success.
To find out how to publish your book, your way, and have it available
worldwide, visit us online at www.trafford.com/10510*

 www.trafford.com

North America & international
toll-free: 1 888 232 4444 (USA & Canada)
phone: 250 383 6864 ♦ fax: 250 383 6804 ♦ email: info@trafford.com

The United Kingdom & Europe
phone: +44 (0)1865 487 395 ♦ local rate: 0845 230 9601
facsimile: +44 (0)1865 481 507 ♦ email: info.uk@trafford.com

10 9 8 7 6 5 4 3 2 1

I would like to thank my dear wife Sharon for her assistance in the publication of this book. I also extend thanks to Ruth Norskog and Kent Douglass for their help.

-ONE-

China March 1862

Hunan Province

Tai-pan Territory

S TIFFLY DISMOUNTING HIS proud steed, the soldier tossed the reins and a large coin to a young boy and glanced up at the familiar high wall surrounding the palace of the Governor-General. After rubbing his horse on its neck and patting the boy on the head, he turned and strode purposefully across a short, narrow wooden bridge and through an open gate. He entered a large courtyard crowded with people waiting a turn for an audience with the Governor-General.

As expected, two husky military guards challenged him. When they noted his rank they saluted, right arms upraised at the elbow, palms forward. They then began disarming the superior officer. One took his short wide-bladed battle sword, while the other patted him down searching for hidden weapons. He wore thick leather armor with metal plating, a knee-length skirt of overlapping leather with metal straps, and a black pleated tunic and trousers—the standard Chinese military uniform, which the guards checked thoroughly.

The taller of the two guards asked, "Why have you come?"

The officer removed his tightly fitting metal helmet then placed a hand inside his tunic. The younger, shorter guard removed a sword from its sheath and fell into a defensive stance. "Hold," laughed the officer, "I bring only a letter." He retrieved a small paper from under his tunic and handed it to the taller guard. He quickly scanned it and said to the other, "It's a personal summons from the General himself." He told the officer, "Follow us sir." After pushing through the crowd, they were soon jogging up a short flight of stone steps to a small iron door leading into the palace.

One of the guards banged on the door with the hilt of his sword. There came the metallic scraping of an inner bolt sliding open. A moment later, the door opened a crack and an eye peered out at them. The guard passed the letter through the gap in the door, after which the door swung open to allow the officer entrance. The two guards remained outside. Once the military officer passed through the portal, the servant slammed the door shut behind him. The servant stated curtly, "Wait here," and crossed the room to disappear through a door at the opposite side of the enormous admittance hall.

Glancing around the hall as he waited, the military man was awed at the ostentatious display spread before him. The floor was of highly polished multihued stone, seamlessly inlaid with artistic Chinese icons of dragons, fish and celestial objects. Vivid tapestries, embroidered with gold and silver thread, covered the walls. Masterfully painted scenes of battling warriors and beautiful women covered the high-domed ceiling. The windowless room was aglow with countless small lamps affixed to the walls. The lamps burned an exotic smokeless fuel known only to the Chinese. The scene was intimidating. Any person, be he diplomat, warlord or peasant, could not help but be humbled by this overwhelming exhibition of wealth and power.

The door at the far side of the hall reopened and the clerk motioned for the officer to enter. As he passed the threshold, he entered an even grander hall. It was cavernous—one obviously designed for the use of hundreds of persons at once. But the officer's attention was drawn not to the décor of the room but to a silken-carpeted platform a foot of so above the floor. Long wooden tables flanked it, manned by several clerks or records keepers who shuffled through stacks of papers in front of them. The officer paid little attention to them. The man who caught his eye sat in a throne-like chair upon the platform—Zeng Gudfan, the Governor-General of Tai-pan. Tai-pan's borders extended over a hundred miles in every direction from this palace city of Cantoo.

The Governor-General was clad in an elegant, flowing Chinese kimono of brilliant red shimmering silk, with Chinese scenes embroidered with gold thread. A heavy black leather belt about his waist held a short, engraved wide-blade sword inlaid with gold, silver and precious gemstones. The Governor-General's head protruded above the high, stiff collar. It was the only visible part of his body—the sleeves of his kimono even covered his hands.

The soldier studied the ruler with interest. The Governor-General had once saved his life. Now the ruler was an elderly, thin-faced man with a narrow gray mustache circling his mouth and running downward until it joined at the tip of his chin with a long, pointed beard. Gray, nearly white hair hung in two long tight braids at the back of his head. His eyes were hard and dark, and nearly intermeshed with his bushy, cascading eyebrows. Yet hard as they appeared, the eyes sparkled with a hypnotic aura, which bespoke an almost mystic power.

The officer was uncertain what to do. Should he bow, approach the throne, and announce his name and errand? Fortunately, he did not have to make the decision. The Governor-General looked up after reading the letter and in a shrill singsong voice said, "Captain Chang, my friend," motioning the captain to approach. "It is such a pleasure to see you again. Military life must agree with you. If all my soldiers looked as fit as you I think I could conquer the world." Chuckling, he continued, "It's been what, fifteen years since that terrible day that I carried you out of your burning house and pulled the arrow from your leg?"

"Almost to the day, sir," answered Captain Chang.

"I am amazed at you. As I recall, you were the only one from your village who survived. Your parents and over two hundred men, women, and children slaughtered, and for what? Those murderous bandits knew that a village such as yours had no valuables to steal—only a few scrawny animals. Those were hard times. Things in our country are vastly improved thanks to loyal soldiers like you." Chang lowered his eyes in humility.

Zeng Gudfan continued, "I was the same rank back then as you are now, a captain in the army. But I had commanded a mere thirty troops. With such a paltry force, we were expected to police the entire territory. Hah! It was an impossible task. The man who ruled us was more concerned with his own pleasure than the welfare of his people. I swore that day that I would improve the way our country worked, and

I did. I took the throne from him, formed a functional military force and the rest is history. Our farmers, merchants and peasants are much safer now to carry on their business without the fear of bandits, soldiers or warlords wiping them out."

"Yes, sir," was all Chang could think to say.

"I called you here my friend, to ask a favor of you. It may delay your military career temporarily, but I assure you that you will lose no seniority or promotions while you are gone."

Chang realized his audience was nearly over when the Governor-General motioned for his servant to admit another person to the throne room. "Captain Chang, I have many other people to see today so regrettably, I must end our discussion. Nevertheless, I assume you will perform my bidding."

"Of course General, my life is yours to command. I only hope I am able to perform the task, whatever it might be."

The General studied him closely before saying, "I never doubted that you would. And do not fret. I know you are well qualified for this assignment." Zeng pointed at a man sitting at the table to his right. "My minister, whom I think you know, will provide you with the details and make all of the arrangements. Until I see you again be careful my friend."

"Thank you sir," said Chang, and bowed his head before leaving.

The minister of external and internal affairs Li Wong gathered a stack of papers in his arms before he approached. "Follow me," he told Captain Chang. He led Chang through a small doorway at the rear of the throne room. "Your military duties must keep you very busy," the minister said with a touch of annoyance. "Your mother worries about you." They walked through a narrow hallway and into a spacious room where several people sat busily reading, writing reports or filling out forms.

"I have been inspecting troop outposts along our borders. I just returned to my barracks this morning and was given the summons to see General Gudfan. I planned to visit you and mother at home this evening."

Li Wong tossed the papers he carried onto a large desk, and sat in a chair at the desk. "Please sit," he said. Chang sat in a large chair with thick cushions. Li Wong continued in a softer tone, apparently appeased. "I know you're a busy man but you should see your mother as often as you can. The day may come when you will never be able to visit her again."

"I know and I understand. Thank you for your concern." After a short pause, Chang asked, "What is this new assignment the General mentioned?"

"You will soon be leaving China for quite some time."

"Leave China?" asked Captain Chang. "Are we going to war?"

"No," Li Wong chuckled, "nothing as serious as that." He picked up and rang a small brass bell from a corner of his desk. A servant ran into the room almost instantly. "Tea," ordered the minister. After the servant hurried from the room, Wong leaned back in his chair said, "Listening to your talk with our General reminded me that it has indeed been a long time since that terrible day you lost your family. Father, mother and what—four brothers and sisters?" Chang nodded his affirmation. "Those bandits were savages. If it is any condolence to you, we caught and killed all thirty of them.

"I was a young man then, about your age when General Gudfan, Captain Gudfan it was then, led me and the few loyal troops we had to try to rescue your village from those bandits. We got there too late. They had already ransacked and set fire to all the huts, and killed everyone for a few goats, chickens and bags of rice. It was a miracle you survived. When Gudfan carried you from of the burning hut, you had a bloody arrow in your leg. I thought you were dead. My young wife Zeo nursed you back to health. She tended your burns and leg wound. She also begged me to adopt you as one of our sons. Adopting you was one of my better decisions. We did not want you to forget the family of you birth, so we wanted you to keep your birth surname, Chang. Still, your mother and I are very proud of you. You have accomplished much more than any of the sons born to us have done, and you did it early in life. Our other sons have not been worth the food we put in their mouths all these years. But you..."

A knock came at the door. Li bid the person enter. The servant returned with the tea and, after placing a tray on the desk, was quickly dismissed with a wave of the minister's hand. As the scent of the warm tea filled the room, Chang suddenly realized how dry his throat felt after traveling the dusty road on his horse. He took a sip of the liquid, and had to force himself to keep from gulping it. He sighed contentedly.

"Your mother," Li began to speak again, "is wise. Probably more wise than I. She knew our other sons would not take kindly to your adoption, and she was right. Your brothers bullied you from the very beginning. That is why we sent you away to school in England almost immediately. We did not want our sons to drive you away permanently. Then we sent you to the University and to the military academy in England. We wanted you to have the finest education possible. And you did not disappoint us."

"But father I..." Chang tried to protest.

"No. I speak the truth. You did more than just graduate. You excelled academically. The European weapons development reports you sent are of great interest to us. China would be helpless if we had to fight with our bows and arrows against rifles. The English methods of casting iron for large cannons and the simple task of rifling the inner barrel of a weapon to increase its accuracy are so simple my weapon makers are already imitating them.

"Enough reminiscing, I'm sure you're wondering why you were chosen for this mission, what it is, and where."

"Yes father, I am."

Leaning back in his chair Li Wong idly twirled a pen in his hand. After a few moments of silence he tossed his pen on his desk, looked over at Chang and said, "To accomplish what we need requires a person with unique talents. He must be honest beyond question, militarily minded, and fluent in speaking, reading and writing English. It was my staff that dictated these requirements and your name topped the list of candidates."

"But father," Chang protested, I am needed here to help protect China.

"My son, I approved their choice. I know of no one better qualified. We need you for this task. To help you understand the necessity of this mission let me give you some background as to how we finance our government. The money to pay all government workers necessary to keep Governor-General Zeng in power comes from our people. The Emperor of all China in Bejing, collects taxes from our people too. He sends his collectors out right after harvest and takes half the harvest from our farmers, and the merchants fare no better. Half of their profits also go to the emperor. He is supposed to give us, our local government, the funds we need to function, but he never does. He only gives us a fraction of what we need. We cannot tax our people more or there would be a revolution."

"Yes, I see the problem," answered Chang.

"Years ago, shortly after the emperor assigned the Governor-General to govern this territory, I realized our most valuable and abundant raw material was our people. Some of the countries to our south were desperately in need of laborers to work their large rubber and coconut plantations. I recruited and organized several labor teams from among our peasants and engaged them to work for the plantation owners. This generated much-needed money to keep our government from bankruptcy."

Chang fidgeted, uneasy about where the discussion was leading.

"It didn't take long," Wong continued, "before other affluent countries approached me. They also wanted to hire our workers for their construction projects roads. I created a volunteer labor force using several teams of ten people each. To join a team each person had to be willing to work anywhere needed for a period of five years. I give each volunteer a significant sign-on bonus, pay all travel expenses, provide a decent wage and give another large bonus when the assignment is complete. Workers collect half their wages monthly, with the other half going into an account that they collect when they return. If they should die, which happens all too often, the earnings go to their families. The workers become wealthy members of their villages. Every village has a pool of volunteers, far more than I can use."

"That is very interesting, but what has it to do with me?" Wong glanced at him sharply. "I am sorry father. Forgive my rudeness. Please continue."

"As I said, each labor team consists of ten men, one of whom is chosen by the others as team leader. The leader's word is law for the team. He also has the power to replace any malcontent or troublemaker on his team. Every six months the leader must be reconfirmed or a new leader is selected. Recently our most profitable working area has been in the gold fields of western America, where we recovered an incredible amount of gold from the state called California. New gold fields are discovered there quite frequently. I formed and sent a great many labor teams to work in the American gold fields as independent miners or as paid laborers for American mine owners.

"Our Chinese gold miners have become the most skillful and experienced miners in the world. I sent many to schools for education. These gifted people become geologists and mining engineers second to none. They travel wherever needed to advise our people where to mine and to teach new mining methods.

"The white European mine owners skim what gold they can off the top gravels only, then thinking it is a "played out," as they say, they quite willingly sell their mines to us. We regularly recover a hundred times more gold from their abandoned mines then they do.

"The white men resent our Chinese workers who remain independent and secret. We do not mingle much with them and we try to keep a low profile. We police our own, and anyone who gets out of line is replaced immediately. All of our workers are required to learn to understand and speak English. If they also learn to read and write the language, they receive even greater rewards for their efforts.

"We instruct our people not to let the Americans know they understand English. They speak only Chinese among themselves. They even use one of our interpreters when we need to communicate with the Americans. It is surprising what we learn from them when they think we don't understand a word of English. Of course," he continued, "It didn't take long for the other governors and warlords in China, who were as strapped for money as we were, to begin sending their own workers abroad to obtain what we call emperor-free money. Some did well, but most did not until they realized my method for obtaining volunteer, not conscript laborers, worked best.

"The first few years were very chaotic with one warlord fighting another for location, territory and power. In fighting was a detriment to us all. I envisioned the time when our battles would cause our exclusion from America. I arranged a conference among all the governors and warlords and convinced them we had to work cooperatively or all would be lost."

Chang poured himself more tea as Wong went on. "We worked out an agreement that has succeeded beyond expectations, creating what we call the China Cooperative. Those who joined our cooperative contribute money and men, and we vote on any expenditures or policy concerning our Chinese laborers such as where, how many, and whose people we place in each area. Holding the entire thing together are a number of well-educated, intelligent men who administer the policies and have absolute authority over the areas they administer. We call them tongs. In every city, mining district, or area that we have large numbers of laborers working, we purchase small tracts of land and construct buildings to house up to twenty people. We call them tong houses. One person in each area, who has no particular loyalty to any one governor or warlord, governs as tong. His word is law to all the Chinese people in the area, even to the extent of execution if necessary. He selects people to serve as agents in administering the area. They buy or lease mines and assign labor teams to work them by consecutive number to prevent favoritism. The same system applies for construction sites, farms and anywhere else that we have workers.

"In America, our headquarters and number one tong is located in the port city of San Francisco. All people and equipment leaving or returning to China pass through the San Francisco tong for accountability and transportation arrangements. All the gold the teams recover goes to him first. There the agents check to ensure all is satisfactory before shipping it to me. I have never lost an ounce of gold insofar as I am aware. This is where we get most of the money we need to fund the Tai-pan government, but recently several things have occurred that might jeopardize the American operations."

"And this is where you need me," interjected Chang.

"Yes my son. I need you to investigate. Our Montana tong has not heard from two of my teams in several months and he fears foul play. Sniff around, learn what you can about the missing teams, and keep me updated on anything that might affect our operations there. One recent report advises of a civil war in eastern America over slavery, which developed into a full-scale conflict. Learn how big a conflict it is and if other nations are involved I want to know the types of weaponry used, and how the conflict will affect our western operations. I will provide a list of all my people you should contact.

"My ship sails from Hong Kong to San Francisco in four days. You will accompany two new labor teams I am sending over there to replace those I lost. Do you have any questions?"

"Yes, father. Is the ship your own?"

Li Wong chuckled and said, "The General and I own four ships with two more being built. We began our endeavor with a single ship, a fine American clipper that we bought very inexpensively. It was one of hundreds of ships abandoned in the San Francisco Bay after the discovery of gold in America. The crews contracted a malady they call gold fever, and left the ships in droves.

"I once made a trip to America and when I saw the abandoned ships, I realized that if we sent our own people by ship it would save us much in transportation fees. We saved so much money that the general and I purchased three more ships in short order. I hire European captains and officers, but the other crewmembers are Chinese. We charge our people a transportation fee to cross the ocean in either direction. We also export tea, silk and other goods to America, and bring back lumber, iron and other resources we need in China. It has become very profitable. We send all gold on our ships. There are very few people even here in China who know of this. Only our number one tong and his people in San Francisco know the vast amounts of gold we transport. I am sure that the crews on the ships suspect what is in the heavy boxes they load into the ship's strong room, but we tell them it is lead to try to satisfy their curiosity.

"Go and check out of your barracks, then visit your Mother for a day or two. You must not stay longer because it will take you two days to get to the ship in Hong Kong."

-TWO-

NORTH AMERICA AUGUST 1862

MONTANA TERRITORY

BLACKFOOT COUNTRY

CLIMBING SLOWLY AND quietly up the steep, wet and slippery sagebrush-covered slope, the man glanced down occasionally to study his two horses tethered in the willows below. They stood with their backs to the breeze, browsing at the brush within reach. They often lifted their heads to sniff the air for an unusual scent, ears stiffly erect as they heard an unusual noise. Once they determined a noise non-threatening, their ears resumed their swiveling scan. Each ear worked independent of the other but both locked onto any noise detected by either.

The man trusted his horses' ability to detect threats long before he could. The horses detected and alerted him to a faint odor of smoke as he rode at a trot up this narrow valley. He followed the tracks of a herd of horses driven by about a dozen Blackfoot warriors. The Blackfoot stole the horses the day before from the Shoshone at Fort Hall, a small army post located on the Snake River at the junction of the Oregon-California immigrant road some sixty miles to the south. Somehow, he had to recover and return the horses to the Shoshone before a full-scale war erupted between the two tribes. He planned to follow and overtake the Blackfoot before they arrived at their village twenty miles north. He hoped to trade for or purchase the stolen horses with the promise of gifts, horses, blankets, and perhaps even some guns that he had stored at the Fort Hall trading post. It had taken him nearly a month to stock several wagonloads of gifts to present the Indians in exchange for their promise not to kill or harass the white men traveling through their country on the nationwide immigration road. The tactic worked well until the new gold rush in the Northwest Territory flooded the area with greedy gold miners, and the gamblers and bandits who preyed on them. New gold mines seemed to pop up everywhere. The rough and ready miners thoroughly disrupted the Indians' ancient way of life.

Further complicating his peacekeeping efforts, the Shoshone had formed a large war party to recover the stolen horses. The trader sat on a powder keg with a short fuse. If the two tribes went to war over a couple of dozen horses it could stir up the other tribes in the territory and all hell would break loose.

From atop a steep ridge he saw the tracks of horses leading in from the south. They passed around the base of the ridge and through a small camp on a narrow flat next to a streamlet. Piles of rock and gravel beside the stream made it obvious that this was a gold miners' setup. A wisp of smoke arose from the camp, and remnants of torn cloth fluttered in the breeze. The horses' tracks led north from the camp and continued along the bank of the stream until they disappeared into clusters of brush and trees. Looking south, he could neither see nor hear any sign of the Shoshone warriors. He was convinced that the Blackfoot were long gone, taking with them whatever booty they had found—horses, weapons and probably a scalp or two.

After descending the hill, the man slowly rode the perimeter of the campsite studying the jumble of tracks left by horse and man. He searched for clues as to what had recently taken place. He was unable to determine how many gold miners had been in camp when the horses stampeded through and he wondered if any escaped the Indian onslaught. Probably not. The Blackfoot most certainly slaughtered anyone not trampled by the horses.

It must have been a scene from hell to the miners. The horses were likely upon them before they could get out of bed. Their night guard might have sounded an alarm, if they had a night guard, but they may have still been asleep when disaster struck. Actually, he thought, it was highly unusual for the Indians to fight at night, but they would do it if they had little chance of losing. They believed that if they were killed in a fight at night they couldn't find the happy hunting grounds in the dark.

Dismounting, he studied the scene, noting the footprints among the horse tracks. Some were made by moccasin-clad feet, but others were a real enigma. The prints were not the unmistakable boot print of white men, but of strange flat-soled shoes.

As he neared the still-smoldering fire pit, bile arose in the back of his throat. A pile of mutilated, bodies lay intertwined as they roasted in the smoldering fire. He fought down the nausea as he levered the corpses from the fire for a closer look. His efforts were impeded because the bodies had coalesced into one. Using a second pole, he was able at last to pry one body loose from the others. The body appeared to be that of an oriental man, perhaps Chinese. This, at least, explained the strange sandal-like prints in the camp. Untangling the entire gruesome mass of bodies, he determined that there were ten bodies, all killed, scalped and incinerated. They may even have lost their scalps while alive and conscious.

The trading post operator felt a twinge of guilt upon thinking that he might have somehow prevented this massacre if he had tried harder to catch up with the Blackfoot warriors he had been trailing all day and night. If the Indians knew about the camp, then this was a planned attack. The Blackfoot Indians knew the value the white man placed on the yellow metal. They also knew that a good trader could exchange a handful of gold for a good gun, powder, bullets and even a horse.

If the Indians simply blundered into the camp, they had still gone out of their way to slaughter and scalp the miners and loot the camp. The entire raid had likely taken place within minutes. Now they were rich in horses and fine prime scalps, and probably gold, and were continuing their journey toward their village an hour or so away.

The trader saw a bucket lying nearby. He retrieved it and filled it with water from the stream to dowse the smoldering fire. Sliding down the steep muddy bank to the rocky streambed, he scooped up a bucket of water. As he carried it up the bank, he heard a low moaning coming from somewhere upstream. He drew his six-shooter and walked as quietly as possible upstream. He approached a pile of dirt where the bank had caved in and saw a man's foot protruding from one side of the mound, and a head from the other.

Grasping the foot, the trader heaved, extracting a man from under the mound. Turning the victim face up, he brushed the mud and dirt from the man's face. The trader squeezed the man's jaws open and dug a plug of mud from his mouth. Seeing the victim gasp, the trader rolled him face down, and pushed on his back until the victim began coughing. The trader propped the victim against the bank. The trader splashed a little water over the victim's face, and the victim's eyelids fluttered open. Squatting down beside him the trader said, "Well, little feller, welcome back to the land of the living. Do you know English or just Chinaman talk?"

The Chinaman looked at him and weakly said, "I speak good English and also Chinaman talk."

"Well now," the white man chuckled, "I reckon there ain't nothing I can't stand more than a smart-alecky Chinaman. I'd like to stop and jawbone a might longer, but we ain't got the time. We got to get a'going, else'n we're both gonna wind up under that there pile of mud."

"My people, did they get away?"

"I hates to tell you this," the trader replied, "but all of your friends is dead and if we don't make tracks on out of here we're gonna be joining 'em. Come on, I got me a couple of horses up yonder." The two stumbled up the bank to the horses, the trader helping the Chinaman along. The trader grabbed the reins of his packhorse and mounted the other. He then reached down and pulled the Chinaman up behind him. Then they headed out.

An hour later, still riding double, the two men rode down a shallow gully leading to the streambed. After crossing the stream, they continued upstream through a brushy area of dense willows and into a small grassy clearing where they halted and dismounted. As he uncinched his saddle the white man said, "Must be time for introductions. My name is Zeb. What do you go by?" he asked as he pulled the saddle off the horse.

The Chinaman said, "My name is Chang." The horse jerked the reins out of Zeb's grasp. As Zeb regained the reins, Chang asked, "Do you need help?"

"No," Zeb replied, "but if these horses go under, so do we. We can let 'em graze fer awhile, then we'll see if we can sneak up out of this creek bottom without being seen." Zeb led the horses to the stream to drink then tied them loosely, allowing them to feed on the tall bottom grasses nearby. After he finished with the horses, he climbed a small hill to check the area. He looked around, returned and said, "Don't see nothing coming yet, so get what rest you can." Zeb stretched himself out on the ground, using the saddle as a pillow, and was immediately asleep.

Chang studied the white man who was about six feet, lithesome but not thin, dressed in a buckskin jumper with what appeared to be tight military wool trousers, faded and stained with use. His feet sported calf-high moccasins, and he wore a wide military belt strapped about his waist. A long knife in a beaded leather sheath hung in front of his left hip and a similar large beaded leather pouch hung over his right hip from a narrow strap looped over his shoulder. A wide-brimmed gray hat drooped forward over his neck-length hair. His face sported a short well-trimmed beard and a long droopy moustache. A slight tinge of gray appeared at the temples. He appeared to be in his mid-thirties. Chang had already noticed Zeb's military bearing and authority of speech.

It was nearly dark when Zeb awoke, glanced at the cloudy gray sky and approached the horses. He saddled the black horse they had been riding double, and loaded his meager supplies on the packhorse. Zeb tightened up the saddle cinch and looked both horses over carefully. He then reached into his pack, withdrew a tightly rolled blanket, tossed it to Chang and said, "Here put this on. Ain't going to help much but it might cut the wind and warm you up a mite. Rain's starting up, but it don't look like it'll last. It sure ain't gonna help us none. Ain't gonna be enough to wash out our tracks."

Zeb mounted, pulled Chang up behind him and rode out of the creek bottom. They followed a ridge leading into the foothills, being careful to stay below the crest to prevent a silhouette against the skyline. After a few miles, they turned up a narrow gully to the ridge crest and came to a halt. "Well," Zeb said, "might as well hole up here. It's about as good a spot as any. The rain stopped so it'll dry as soon as the sun's up."

After they dismounted, Zeb removed the packs and saddle, and led the horses down the slope several feet. He tied them in a stand of scrubby trees and returned to the ridge top near Chang. Chang had dozed off with the blanket around him. Waking with a start, Chang saw the sun just peeking over the horizon. Zeb was lying belly down, peering over the ridge crest. Chang crawled up beside him. Hearing him approach Zeb whispered, "Take a look yonder. There is them Injuns just about where I figured they would be."

Chang saw the stream far below. Beside the mouth of the gully was a large group of mounted horsemen. Zeb handed Chang a battered telescope and said, "Here, take a good look at this. Tough looking bunch of critters all painted up like they is. Believe me, if they catch up to us we ain't gonna do no laughing."

Focusing the telescope, Chang was spellbound by the small group of riders with strange patterns painted on their face and chests. They were armed with long spears trailing fluttering feathers in the breeze, quivers of arrows, and short bows slung on their backs. A few had long guns resting across their thighs. "Unbelievable," he muttered to himself, then looking at Zeb said, "So those are the American Indians I've heard so much about. Are they the ones who killed my people?"

"No, them folks down there are Shoshone, a mean bunch of when they get all painted up like that. See that varmint? The one with the feathers pointed down on his head? That's Chief Bird Tracker. That critter can track a bird in the air. They know we either came up this way or went up the gully on the other side. They're arguing about it now so I guess we fooled 'em some." Zeb took the telescope and studied the aborigines. He then said, "Bird Tracker is sure we came up this way but the others ain't convinced. I think they're getting a little spooked. I don't blame 'em, we're right in the middle of Blackfoot country."

The horsemen milled around in obvious confusion for a minute or two. Then Bird Tracker slid off his horse and faced the ridge where Zeb and Chang hid. The chief raised his spear above his head and shook it violently, screaming wildly. He remounted his horse, turned and galloped back downstream followed by his companions. Zeb chuckled and said, "That there was a challenge. He knows we're up here somewhere and he aims to get us next time."

"How do you know what they were saying?"

"Injuns use hand signs to talk when they are on the prowl or when parleying with other tribes. Talking with hand signs is a common language known to every Injun in the whole country. Something you got to learn if you're going to do any dealing them."

Backing down the slope he said, "Keep a watch on the horses while I take a look around and make sure them critters ain't just trying to outfox us. If I get bushwhacked and don't show up in a couple of hours you head north. It's about three days to Bannack," then picking up his rifle and tossing his revolver to Chang he went back down the slope, staying hidden in the gully.

Chang awoke with a start, glanced up at a cloudless sky with the sun directly overhead and realized he had dozed for several hours. The horses tethered below showed no sign of alarm so he knew he was in no immediate danger. He opened Zeb's pack and found a skin water bag tied to the outside of the pack. As he took a swig, he heard a faint click above him. He glanced up, directly into the round bore of a rifle. His eyes swept up the gun barrel to a grinning face, which spoke, "Bang you're dead." Then Zeb lowered the rifle and proceeded downhill until he stood beside the shocked Chinaman.

"Well, now," Zeb laughed, "if I was an Injun I would be hanging your scalp on my belt right now. We can forget about them Injun varmints fer now. They done hightailed it back to Snake River country. I figure we best hold up here a spell so you can rest then you can get back to Bannack where you can find some of your China fellers to help you."

Setting down near a small smokeless fire, Chang leaned back against a large rock and said, "I owe you my life. I wish I could repay you for the trouble I've caused."

Zeb replied, "I'm a bit curious as to just what in the hell you Chinamen was doing down here in the middle of Blackfoot country. You set yourselves up as Injun bait that not even their squaws could resist. If the Blackfoot hadn't got ya, the Shoshone probably would have."

"Well," Chang answered, "We never had any trouble with the Indians before. I guess we have been so cautious with the white men that we ignored the Indians. I should have investigated the Indians hereabouts to see if they are hostile so I could warn my people. Now I need to recover their remains and return them to China to be buried with their ancestors, as is our custom."

Zeb finished roasting some crisp jerky strips, "This will fill your belly for awhile, at least until I can get us some fresh meat, I don't mean to pry into a feller's private affairs but I'm mighty curious as to how long your people have been mining in this here area? The Bannack and Virginia City diggings ain't been there very long. Matter of fact, the whole of Idaho and Montana is new mining territory."

Chang replied, "I left China several months ago accompanying twenty of our people coming to work in the Montana gold fields. We landed at San Francisco then boarded another ship that took us north to a town called Portland. There we bought horses and supplies and trailed through the mountains to Bannack and Virginia City."

"And you just done all this on your own?"

"My employer, a general, sent me over here to America on a mission for our country."

"Are you a spy?"

"No, America is not our enemy. The general is responsible for all the Chinese people here in western America. Twenty of our people disappeared and I came to find out what happened to them. The general also heard rumors of a civil war being fought back east. He wishes to know more of the details."

"What's that got to do with gold mining?"

Chang felt his face flush. He hadn't wanted to reveal anything about the Chinese mining operations. "Gold mining?" he asked, stalling for a moment to think.

"Yeah, gold mining. I could tell what you fellas was doing by the way your camp is set up. That's also why them Injuns killed your pals, they was after your gold."

Zeb had saved his life and he seemed trustworthy so Chang decided to be honest with him. "Yes," Chang admitted, "we were gathering gold to send back to China. I am supposed to observe the Chinese mining operations to make sure they are in order. When I got to Virginia City our Chinese foreman there, called our tong, informed me they had found all of our missing people. They died in an avalanche in the mountains north of there.

"I have been helping our people where I could, checking and reporting their work locations, what supplies they needed and trying to make myself useful. Our Montana tong sent this mining group to prospect the stream where you found us for gold. I arrived at their camp after riding all night. I unloaded supplies from my two packhorses and led them down to the stream to drink when those Indians charged. The next thing I remember is you beating on my back. We were concerned about the white bandits and robbers who terrorize the area, robbing and murdering isolated miners, holding up stagecoaches and supply wagons. None of us gave the Indians much thought. The few Indians we saw near the gold camps seemed peaceful enough. We didn't think they lusted for gold like the white men do."

Zeb leaned back, enjoying the warmth of the sun and said, "The Injuns discovered that they can buy anything they want if they have enough of the yellow metal, but they don't search for their own. They just steal it after someone else finds it fer 'em. So what's a Chinaman soldier doing here in America?"

"I never said I was a soldier," said Chang, taken aback.

"You said you worked fer a general. Anyways, I figured you fer a soldier from the way you walk. I figure you is a officer most likely. Seems like one soldier always recognizes another when he sees one."

"You got me, yes I am a soldier, a captain with the army of the Hunan Province in China."

"No big surprise there. Yet you say you ain't a spy?"

"No," laughed Chang, "I am most definitely not a spy."

"Just gotta make sure. By the way, can you use that knife you've got hanging behind your back? I noticed it when I pulled you out of the dirt pile." The knife zipped past Zeb's ear before the American had a chance to react. A dull thud and rustling sound came from behind him. Zeb whirled and saw a huge rattlesnake thrashing furiously, pinned to the ground by the long tapered knife. Looking back at Chang he slowly stood saying, "Looks like that answer's yes. Thank ye." Zeb retrieved the knife, gutted and skinned the snake. "You probably saved my life, and now we got meat too. Won't even have to do any hunting today." Wiping the blade clean he threw the knife back toward Chang, imbedding it in the ground an inch from Chang's big toe. "Good knife, well-balanced."

Chang looked at him and said, "Now you know how fate brought me to this place but why are you here?"

"I guess fate is a good way to put it. It does make a feller wonder don't it? I come from a place back east called Illinois. Never knew my Ma, she died having me. Lived with kin folks while my Pa went off trapping. When I was about ten, my Pa took me with him when he hired on to the Hudson Bay, a British fur trapping outfit, and we came out here and trapped furs and traded with the Injuns. We got to know 'em all. After a few years he got tired of trapping and we went over to Californey and chased around the goldfields. We hit it pretty lucky, me and him. Found a lot of gold before he got himself shot by road agents. Them varmints ambushed and held us up, only pa didn't do too good at being held up and they shot his arm off. One-armed Pa, he sets hisself up a miners' supply business in San Francisco. I joined up in the army for a few years. I didn't want to settle down and sell gold pans and shovels to a bunch of runaway sailors."

Zeb filled his pipe with tobacco and lit it with an ember from the small fire. He took a couple of puffs and, satisfied it was working, pointed the pipe stem at Chang and said, "Things here in America has got real confusing lately and I don't think nobody can sort it out. I went back east awhile back, figured to join back up in the army but couldn't stomach shooting at other white folks.

"I went and visited an old friend I grew up with—Abe Lincoln— he's the head honcho over all of America now. He talked me into going to work for him, deputized me as Federal Marshal. I got to report to him about what's going on out here in the west, same as you report to your general. Chang must have looked a little puzzled, because Zeb then said, "I best tell you how this country works. Started off with a bunch of pilgrims from Europe colonizing an area along the American east coast. They set up their own government, colonies they called 'em. Democratic ones. That means all the folks who lived there got to vote on who rules them. They divided up all the land around those colonies and called 'em states. The governors of all the states got together and voted in a president. He's kind of like your Emperor I suppose, excepting all of these politicians have to tow the line 'cause they get voted in or out every few years.

"Things grew bigger of course, with more settlers making more states. It went along pretty well fer awhile, but now some of the southern folks figured they ain't getting a fair shake. They don't think they can keep their farms and plantations going without some unpaid help from their slaves who was kidnapped from Africa. The northern folks don't figure that nobody should make slaves. The folks in the south, they wants to split off and make their own separate country. My pal Abe and the other northern folks want to keep us all together as one nation. One thing done led to another with each side raising an army and squaring off. It sure could turn into a hell of a bloody war and I ain't got no idea of how it's going to end up.

"The United States of America claims all the territory south of Canada and north of Mexico. Both of these countries know we're kind of pre-occupied in the east and are trying to extend their borders a bit while we ain't watching. To top it off, a big bunch of people has started settling and claiming a large territory just south of us near a large saltwater lake. We call it the Utah territory and they call it the state of Deseret, or Zion. These folks call themselves Mormons. They are Christians but their beliefs is somewhat different than other Christian beliefs, so much so that they was run plum out of the east where they got started. They moved clear out here in the wilderness to get away from everybody so they could be free to worship as they please.

"Old Abe, he asked me to go down and see if these Mormons was a threat to our country figuring we might have to fight them too. I went down and met these folks, found out that they aren't no threat at all, in fact they is the best thing that could have happened for us right now. I got to know their leader, a feller called Brigham Young, one of the best men I ever met. They are all very honest and hard working people. They made farms and ranches out of nothing but dry arid land. They dug ditches, made roads, constructed a big and real pretty capital city, Salt Lake City. I couldn't believe it was all built right there in the middle of a desert.

"They told me what their religious beliefs were, mostly straight out of the Christian Bible, excepting for one thing that caused all their grief with other Christian folks. They figure, like the Injuns do, that you are free to marry up with all the ladies they can afford. Most white folks don't go along with that idea. Don't know why, sounds good to me," he said laughing, "I might just have to join up with 'em someday. These are mostly peace loving folks, but if you get 'em riled up they're tougher than boiled jerky. The whole kit and caboodle will take after you if you do 'em wrong, but they ain't no threat to President Lincoln and our country. Fact is, they sent a bunch of fellers to join the American Army when they was asked, even after they was thrown out of their homes several times in the east.

"Don't want to bore you no more, but my mission here makes more sense if you know a little bit of what's going on. It's absolutely vital to the President's war effort to keep the road open from the west coast to the east to transport the gold mined in Californey to the bankers in New York City. He begs, borrows, sells land and whatever elese he can do to keep the gold shipments coming. It's the only currency other nations will accept from us to buy the arms and supplies we need fer war. Right now, all the dollars we print ain't worth the paper they're printed on. Folks has got to calling 'em Lincoln Skins, good to nobody except as a means to pay our soldiers. Fortunately, most loyal merchants accept 'em, hoping our government will make good on 'em later on after we win the war.

"My job is to deal with the Injuns, try to keep them from closing the coast to coast immigrant road. I have the power to make treaties, bribe, pay, trade and promise anything to ensure they leave the white travelers unharmed. I've had pretty good luck getting most of the tribes who claim the country near the immigrant road to promise to not harm our travelers. It took many trade goods to get their marks on paper. Lately, I've ran into problems with these Injuns around here, the Bannacks, the Shoshone and the Blackfoot. They seemed to be under control for a spell. If I can't get things patched up, the immigrant road is going to be closed fer sure.

"I got the word out to the Shoshone, the Bannack and the Blackfoot to meet me at Fort Hall, a small trading post south of here, for a council and lots of presents from our big white chief. They all came. Chief Washaki of the Shoshone, Chief Pocatello of the Bannacks and the chief of the Blackfoot, named Three Fingers. Things were going pretty well till one of the traders at the Fort traded 'em a keg of whiskey and then all hell broke loose."

Stretching, Chang asked, "So what happened, did they get into a drunken brawl?"

"Worse than that, I gave each tribe a wagonload of goods to divvy out amongst their people. Everyone was gorging themselves on the beef I brought from the fort and having a good time, but when they started drinking the whiskey a little squabble come up when one of the Blackfoot gets mad at a trade he made with one of the Bannacks. Guess he traded a horse for a gun, and the gun had a bent barrel. All of the Blackfoot Injuns tells him a trade is a trade so he loads up that old smooth bore, walks over and shoots the horse he traded away. He says he was shooting at a coyote in the other direction but the dad-blamed bullet flew out the bent barrel and hit the horse. Everyone except the new owner of the horse thought it was pretty funny until he grabs the gun, loads it up and shoots the feller he traded with in the leg. He claimed he was pointing it at the same coyote and sure enough, it shoots crooked so the trade is off and he could have his dead horse back.

"Then one of the other varmints gets the gun, loads it up and throws it on the fire, and said that no one will miss shooting that coyote again. Well," Zeb continued, "the ammo in that gun blew up and killed a Shoshone. Then everyone started shooting at each other. While everyone was hollering, whooping and shooting away, the Blackfoot gathered up their horses, and most of the Shoshone horses too, and hustled on back up here to their own country.

"I took out after the Blackfoot to try and get them Shoshone and Bannack horses back but I guess they figured I was in cahoots with the Blackfoot. The Shoshones rounded up what horses they could find or steal from the folks at the Fort and comes after me and the Blackfoot to get their horses back. I been trying to find the Blackfoot and avoid the Shoshone all at the same time. Them Blackfoot wasn't far ahead of me when they headed into your camp. Must've figured they'd gather up your gold while they were out and about, and collect a few scalps to boot. I think they already know'd about your camp cause they went straight there. So here I am—fair game for every Injun in the territory unless I can unruffle some Shoshone-Bannack feathers with a passel of fancy horse trading."

Zeb wiped off his rifle, checked his powder flask and bullet pouch then looked over each greased bullet patch and percussion cap as he tucked it into a small pocket attached to the pouch. Seeing Chang watching, he said, "If you hope to survive in this country you have to be right the first time. One misfire or bad cast bullet will sure enough do you in. You can only get one shot off at a mad Grizzly or a mean Injun. If you miss you best start running 'cause you ain't got time to load up again."

Standing up and looping the pouches over his shoulder, he picked up his rifle and slipped it into a beaded doeskin case. He said, "Check over the horses while I take a gander." He reached into one of the packs and withdrew a large pistol. Tossing it to Chang he said, "It's loaded and ready to go but don't touch it off unless you have to, there's lots of ears are roaming around these here hills." Then he strode quietly out of camp.

Returning at dusk, Zeb dropped the carcass of a small deer. "Thought you might want a little something to chow on with the rattler," he told Chang. He made sure the horses were content in the grove below. Seeing nothing amiss, he chucked off his gear, leaned his rifle against a nearby rock and was startled to hear a faint click. Spinning around and grabbing for his revolver, he found himself staring directly into the small, mean-looking bore of a pistol. He never cleared leather. A quiet voice said, "Bang, you're dead." Zeb realized the voice came from the grinning face of Chang, who was holding the handgun.

"Well, you're learning. You just might live a mite longer than I figured." Squatting on his haunches, Zeb said, "It's probably best that you get started on your way back up to the Bannack diggings come daylight. You'll find some of your Chinaman folks there. I'm thinking of getting myself on up to the Blackfoot camp and see if I can trade 'em something for them horses they stole. Probably best I don't get there too soon. I need to give them critters some time to do all their lying, bragging, dancing and such. They know, I know, where and how they came by all them horses and scalps and they sure ain't going to want me around telling the truth of it any sooner than they can help it. Might make it a lot easier to dicker with 'em if I'm alone. They might figure I'll be more likely to keep my mouth shut. Maybe I can do my trading and skedaddle."

"In China we call it saving face. I would like to go with you to their camp and try to buy or trade with them for the scalps of my people. It's important to me to return all of their bodies to China for burial with their ancestors so I can save face."

Zeb sat thoughtfully staring into the fire for a few minutes then said, "A man has to do what he has to do. I'll help you all I can but to be right truthful with you, Chang, I don't figure them varmints will part with them scalps. They up their standing in the tribe, even more than horses, kids, dogs, and squaws, in just that order. I don't figure you will ever buy or trade for 'em but you might steal or win 'em somehow. If you want to come along and see what you can do I'll take you with me but it might well be that your hair will join those of your friends hanging on a scalp pole before all is said and done. Fact is, might be both our scalps hanging there."

"No. Not if this endangers your life, I will think of some other way."

"My, my," Zeb replied, chuckling. "Ain't you a formal talker? You sound like them army officers back at the Fort. I don't know what they say half the time so I just saluted to make 'em feel good, then did what I wanted. You take care of your topknot and let me hang on to my noggin as best I can."

Chang laughed and said, "It sounds like your army works the same as mine. The action starts in the middle with the blame going down and the credit going up. If you're willing to take me along I hope I don't give you cause to regret it." Chang took the pistol from his waistband, looked it over and asked, "This hand weapon, I've practiced shooting similar handguns in Europe but nothing quite this big. What caliber is it?"

"This gun uses a .45 caliber bullet the same as my rifle, makes it handy to cast bullets of the same size. You load up each of these holes the same as a rifle. These new percussion caps fit over these here nipples on the back end of the cylinder so when the hammer falls on one of 'em it pops and explodes the powder, blowing the bullet out of the barrel. When you pull back on the hammer, it turns the cylinder to line up the next load.

"It's these little caps that make the new repeater guns possible. They done away with the flint and steel and priming powder to set off the gunpowder charge. Sure makes it a lot easier and faster for folks to kill each other. This here pistol makes lots of noise and lots of smoke and scares the hell out of who you're shooting at, but don't expect to hit nothing over fifty feet. If you're shooting at a buffalo you best not shoot till you can push the barrel right against its hide." Zeb showed Chang how to take the pistol apart and put it back together again, load it and set the caps then said, "Well, that's about all there is to this pistol, a right handy little weapon."

The next morning as Chang finished roasting several venison strips, Zeb said, "I'll go get the horses then we'll mosey on up to that Blackfoot camp and see what happens. We can ride north and get there in an hour or so."

Their trek wound through the foothills, and they always kept to the lower slopes when possible. Chang pointed to a wisp of smoke on a hilltop far to the left. Zeb nodded and pointed out another column of smoke coming from the top of a ridge to the right. "That's Injun smoke talk," Zeb said. "I don't rightly know how to read it but I figure they is telling everyone where we is at and which way we is going. Best we give the horses a breather," he said while dismounting. "We'll walk a spell 'cause we might need these horses for a fast getaway."

Leading the horses, they went up a draw toward the top of a ridge. There Zeb halted and checked the saddle cinch. He then stated, "Well, Chang, the Blackfoot camp is just over that ridge ahead where you see all that dust and smoke coming up. I reckon we'd best get on with it and see what kind of reception they got in store."

-THREE-

THE SUN WAS behind them when a steep bluff dropped off dead ahead. It fell sharply for several hundred feet before tapering off into a narrow flat valley with a fair-sized river flowing down from the south, forming a natural barrier. Steep cliffs bordered the opposite side of the valley. Chang stood mesmerized at the spectacle below. Hundreds of conical tents haphazardly dotted the valley floor and a large herd of horses was corralled against the cliffs on the far side. From his vantage point, he viewed people milling about while horsemen rode through the camp raising clouds of dust.

"Quite a sight ain't it?" asked Zeb. "Now when we get down there you keep your mouth shut, your ears open and don't do nothing unless I tell you to! They will likely look you over pretty good, but you got to just flat ignore 'em. Eyes open and mouth shut, you hear?"

They rode down the steep slope and across the shallow river then up the other bank and into camp. After pulling up, Zeb and Chang dismounted. Zeb said, "From here on out I got to play it as I see it, and you've got to act like you're a great Chinese Chief just coming to pay 'em a friendly visit. I'll tell you what they say if it's important but if you pay attention you should get the gist of what's going on"

Zeb led the horses while Chang walking alongside. Chang's first impression of the Blackfoot people was complete chaos. After passing between or around the first of the outer-placed lodges, Chang saw hoards of women and children running ahead of them and could hear still others coming up behind. It was bedlam with women calling to each other, children screaming, and dogs everywhere. Dogs of every description were running, barking, darting in to snap at Chang, Zeb and their horses, and yelping as the women or children hit them with clubs or rocks. An aroma of roasting food mixed incongruously with the befouled stench of horses, dogs and humans. It was nearly impossible to avoid stepping in dung, which nearly blanketed the ground.

Stopping and gesturing to several of the bolder women nearby, Zeb spoke to them in a strange guttural language. His hands and fingers bent into various shapes as he spoke. Then he handed the reins of his horses to a couple of the women, and stood watching as they led the horses away. Slowly the women and children disappeared, replaced by lines of young men forming a narrow corridor in front of a large cone-shaped lodge that sat somewhat apart from the others. Chang surmised that lodge belonged to the chief. Three men stood near the entrance to the lodge. They were stiffly erect with folded arms. Each wore a headpiece of brightly colored feathers trailing down from their head to the ground. They wore vestures of soft looking leather shirts with beaded designs, long leather trousers and knee length moccasins. Short leather fringes edged the hems of each article of clothing. The men forming the corridor nearest the lodge were mature-looking warriors who remained alert. The women, children and even the yelping dogs remained behind the warriors.

A few feet in front of the tribal leaders, Zeb stopped, put his rifle on the ground and raised both hands with palms facing forward. He spoke rapidly in the guttural language, which was completely unintelligible to Chang. There was a long silence before one of the Indian leaders spoke with one hand upraised, palm facing Zed and Chang.

Zeb turned to Chang and said, "Well, they invite us to sit and speak but they don't rightly welcome us, and there is a big difference." As they stood facing the tribal elders, a woman lit small fire near the lodge. The elders sat cross-legged beside it. The corridor of warriors shifted as Zeb led Chang to the opposite side of the fire. Zeb sat and motioned Chang to do likewise. The flanking warriors quietly arranged themselves in rows behind them facing the elders.

The tribal leaders stared at Zeb and Chang across the fire for several minutes before one of them arose. He spoke as he gestured toward Zeb and Chang, and toward the hills. Zeb translated, "He asks, what brings Shoots Long Shots—that's me—to the land of the Blackfoot. And who is the man of yellow color with you? Is he your slave, prisoner, or do you bring him as a gift to your brothers, the Blackfoot?"

Zeb whispered to Chang, "Well, here we go, so keep looking like a chief. I'll talk to 'em in hand sign so I can talk to you in English at the same time. Great Chief Three Fingers, chief of the Blackfoot, your brother, Shoots Long Shots, has come to speak to you on important matters. I bring with me a great warrior chief of the yellow men, whose tribe owns all the lands beyond the large salty water and number more than the stars in the late summer night sky. Their land is known as China. This man is a brother of Shoots Long Shots. This Chief wishes to make talk with the great chief of the Blackfoot on matters that do not concern me. The China Chief does not speak the tongue of the Blackfoot and does not understand the hand signs I make. I speak to you on behalf of him, and on behalf of him to you, knowing you can also speak the tongue of the white man."

The Blackfoot Chief stared at Chang for a moment, then said, "I Three Fingers, chief of the Blackfoot, ask his friend Shoots Long Shots, why he speaks with a forked tongue. We are not children. Shoots Long Shots followed my warriors from the trading post as did the Shoshone. The Shoshone are angry with us for taking their horses. We are happy that the Shoshones are angry. My warriors have the scalps of the yellow men. My people are happy. The Shoshone have no scalps and have lost many horses. This yellow man still has a scalp on his head. Did you bring his live scalp as a gift to your brothers, the Blackfoot? My warriors watched Shoots Long Shots and the yellow man hide in the hills. My warriors watched you eat deer and then come to our village. Is the yellow friend of yours a warrior? He walks like a warrior, not like the poisonous white government agents who slither like snakes."

"The yellow man is a warrior in China," answered Zeb. "But he does not come to Blackfoot country as a warrior. He has no weapons and no horse. Why do you say he is the friend of Shoots Long Shots when he is only a yellow man who was alone in the wilderness? I found him and I brung him to talk to you. I have spoken."

Zeb looked at Chang and muttered, "Well he done got us there. Can you handle any weapon besides your knife? We got to show 'em some how that you're a sure enough warrior."

"I've noticed their weapons, the bow and arrow, small axe, knife, lance and clubs. In China, we used these weapons long before the red men came to this country. I assure you I am proficient with all of them."

"Profi...Proficient? I sure hope that means you can use 'em." Zeb spoke to the tribal elders again. "Shoots Long Shots is a brother to the Blackfoot. I have slept many moons with you and I never spoke to you with a forked tongue. I have known this Yellow Chief for very few suns. It is well known that no creature leaves sign on the ground in this land that the Blackfoot can't read. No creature moves in this land that the Blackfoot does not know about. I am here because the Blackfoot have the Shoshone horses. But the Shoshone have all of the trade goods I was to give to you, the Blackfoot, from our Great White Father.

"The Blackfoot do not need the Shoshone horses, but your Blackfoot warriors and your women would rejoice with their gifts of beads and colored cloth and the guns and powder to kill game to feed your people. It would be a big joke on the Shoshone to give me back their horses. You know you could go to their village and steal them back anytime. This would make me and our Great White Father very happy, and the Blackfoot would again be welcome to trade at the trading lodge on the Snake River."

The elders conferred among themselves in obvious disagreement over a solution. After much arguing, Three Fingers again spoke, "We hear what our brother Shoots Long Shots tells us. We know you speak as our brother with a straight tongue. It is true that we have many good horses and do not need these crippled horses we stole from the Shoshone. We would only feed their horses to our dogs, but if our dogs get too hungry we can steal them back. We will give our brother Shoots Long Shots these crippled horses, but only if our Great White Father gives his Blackfoot people many gifts to repay us. To this we have all agreed."

Zeb considered their demands and said, "My brothers make a hard bargain. If I trade you all of the fine and valuable things that you want I will have nothing left to trade to my friends the Crow and the Ute, who might go on the warpath against my white brothers passing through their lands. Would you feel good knowing these, your brothers, would get none of these fine gifts from our Great White Father?"

Again, animated discussion erupted among the chiefs. At last, Chief Three Fingers said, "We feel sorry for our brothers the Ute and the Crow, but they have what they need to survive the great snows. They do not need the fine gifts from the Great White Father. They will not suffer as our people will suffer when our dogs die because they have no Shoshone horses to eat. We love our dogs as we do our children. Our women will mourn loudly when they see their dogs die of hunger."

Zeb whispered to Chang, "Greedy bunch of varmints ain't they?" Then addressing the leaders loudly he said, "Great chiefs, if I give you the gifts you desire I will have no more at the trading fort on the Snake River. The great snows will be gone before more gifts will come here. Our Great White Father who gives you these fine gifts lives far, far away. He is in a war, and cannot send the gifts now. If you take all the gifts, I must tell the Ute and Crow chiefs that the Blackfoot have them. The Crow and the Ute will not be happy with the Blackfoot."

"This is how it must be," answered Chief Three Fingers.

"Then I will do this. Your brother, Shoots Long Shots has heard the wise chiefs speak, and so it is agreed." To Chang he muttered, "Well, I got my job done. Now we got to see what we can do about your problem." Zeb again addressed the chiefs saying; "Now I wish to speak to all the great chiefs of the Blackfoot the words of the Yellow Chief." He told Chang, "You do the talking, but remember some of 'em speak English. Talk straight, they ain't no dummies."

As Chang spoke, Zeb interpreted. "I am Chang, chief of the Chinese people your warriors killed near the river where we camped. Our people did not know the Blackfoot were our enemy. We knew you were watching us gather the yellow metal from the river, but we meant no harm to your people. I had just arrived at our camp. My horse was drinking from the stream when your warriors murdered my brothers and buried me in the mud at the riverbank. Do your Blackfoot warriors consider it brave to kill my brothers who have no weapons and have done you no harm?"

"Careful now," Zeb whispered a warning, which Chang ignored.

"Are your warriors like women who sneak up in the dark and kill their enemies while they are sleeping?" A great murmur arose from the Blackfoot. "I demand that your warriors give me the scalps so that I can return them to their homeland as is the custom of my people."

When Chang stopped speaking, Zeb sighed and told Chang, "I tried to warn you." After Zeb finished interpreting, the chiefs assembled warriors a furor arose among them. Zeb looked at Chang and said, "I think you done talked yourself into a heap of trouble."

Chief Three Fingers stood, waved his angry warriors to silence and folded his arms. His eyes Pierced Chang's through the smoke of the fire. In English he said, "Yellow men did not ask the Blackfoot for permission to come on their land to harvest the yellow metal. Now this yellow man insults all Blackfoot warriors. He say he is a warrior chief, so we will see if he fights like one."

Three Fingers pointed to a huge warrior standing nearby and said, "Claws That

Walk say he pushed the yellow man in the river. He say he has the scalp of another yellow man, but this yellow man's scalp also belong to him because he lost it in the river. He say he will fight the yellow man for the scalp he lost."

Calmly Chang replied, "I agree to the fight, but if I win I claim the scalps of all my people."

After Zeb interpreted, the tribal members laughed. Through the commotion Chief Three Fingers said, "You will fight, but for one scalp only—the scalp taken by Claws That Walk. You must fight one warrior to win one scalp."

Chang nodded. Chief Three Fingers said, "It is agreed. Now talk is over. We eat then watch Claws That Walk take scalp from yellow man." Three Fingers turned and entered the large lodge behind him as two other elders returned to their own lodges. All ignored Zeb and Chang.

Zeb looked at Chang, gripped him on the shoulder and said, "You're sure enough in a bad spot. Maybe I can still talk 'em out of this fight."

"There is no need to talk them out of it, I meant to challenge them. Now what happens?"

"Claws That Walk names the weapon. You will each get similar ones, but it'll be one he thinks gives him an edge. He's one big Injun. Next to him you're a runt. He might decide to fight you with his bare hands. Might just rip your arms and legs off before he takes your scalp. We'll have to wait and see."

Two women emerged from a lodge and handed them each a steaming bowl of a thick stew and a slab of roasted meat. Zeb told Chang, "You best eat up cause you're going to need all the strength you can get." Drums began rumbling a strong steady beat with only a slight but continuous change in the rhythm. Zeb said, "They got their drums talking. They is telling the whole dang territory about the big fight coming up. Trust the Blackfoot to make a big hoo-hah about it. They is just getting warmed up too. The dancing around the scalp pole ought to start any minute. Their figuring your scalp will be hanging there soon."

Chang removed his bulky shirt and the knife that hung between his shoulder blades and tossed them to Zeb. Squeezing the chunk of fat meat he was eating, Chang coated his bare chest, arms and shoulders with grease. He took Zeb's meat and rubbed all the fat and grease he could into his hair, face, and neck until his exposed skin glistened. He then took a handful of dirt and cleaned the grease from the palms of his hands. Right after he finished, the elders returned to the fire. Other tribal members crowded around to get a view of the upcoming fight.

Babbling people, yapping dogs and throbbing drums suddenly stopped as the tall warrior, Claws That Walk, clad only in a breach cloth and moccasins, arrived. Zeb did not need to interpret as the Indian warrior stated in very plain English, "I am Claws That Walk and I come for this yellow man's scalp that I lost at the river." After handing Chief Three Fingers a pair of identical long, heavy knives, Claws That Walk stepped back and stared haughtily around at the assembled people.

Chief Three Fingers arose. Looking at Chang he announced, "The fight will start here," pointing to a spot a few yards away from the fire, "and go where it goes." He handed Chang one of the knives and gave the other to Claws that Walk.

Remembering how Chang's knife pierced the rattlesnake, Zeb felt somewhat relieved to see that knives were the chosen weapons. Chang walked to the spot indicated by the chief as Zeb said, "Good luck!"

Chang replied, "Thank you for your help."

"Help?" Zeb replied. "I think I done killed you when I brung you here. I should of sent you back to Bannack or Virginia City."

The drumming began again as Claws that Walk strode forward. The Indian warrior stopped in front of Chang, made a gesture as if slicing off his scalp and grinned broadly at the crowd. He then dropped into a crab-legged crouch and sidled toward Chang. The Indian held the knife low, blade forward, poised for a stabbing thrust that could easily disembowel Chang.

Chang stood in a half crouch, legs apart, with the knife held in his left hand, blade pointing skyward. He watched the Indian steal forward. A piercing war cry erupted from Claws that Walk as he leaped forward, his knife sweeping upward in a wicked thrust. Chang pivoted on his right leg, tossed his knife from left hand to right as the Indian's knife barely missing him. Faster than the eye could follow, his now empty left palm swept up, striking his foe just below the ear. The Indian dropped like a clubbed rabbit. Chang leapt on Claws that Walk's back, placing the point of his knife against his throat.

All members of the crowd, including Zeb, sat stunned. An eerie silence prevailed as the crowd breathlessly waited to see Chang kill the unconscious warrior. Chang released the Indian's head, which flopped to the ground with a thud. Chang stood up, tossed the knife beside the inert body then turned and strode back toward Zeb. The stunned silence snapped with shouts from the tribal members. Zeb yelled, "Watch out Chang! There's another red varmint coming up behind you."

Chang turned to see another Indian approach, body hideously dabbed and streaked with brightly colored paint and carrying a tomahawk in his hand. The Indian stopped at the unconscious body and scooped up the knife dropped by Claws that Walk.

The warrior yelled something to the chiefs and again silence engulfed the crowd as Three Fingers stood. The chief pointed at Chang then at the Indian holding the knife and tomahawk and spoke in a raised voice. The chief then dropped his arm and looked expectantly at Chang.

Zeb called, "The chief says that Yellow Feather also has the scalp of one of your brothers and he challenges you to take it from him. I think you should back off. You already won one fair and square so don't push your luck."

"Will they give me all the scalps if I don't fight?" Chang asked.

"I doubt it. But is a bunch of hair worth losing your life over?"

Chang considered this and said, "Tell Yellow Feather to give me the knife. He can keep his little axe and the knife of Claws that Walk, but they won't be enough to keep him from joining Claws that Walk lying in the dirt."

Zeb replied, "You're a fast learner of Injun ways but don't get too cocky. These here varmints are born fighters. I don't think Yellow Feather figures to kill you until after he shows off a mite. but don't count on it, he just might try to whack you down right at the git-go."

Zeb looked at Yellow Feather and told him exactly what Chang had just said. A roar of approval swelled from the crowd as Yellow Feather stood, holding the knife of Claws that Walk in one hand and his tomahawk in the other. But the Indian made no attempt to pick up Chang's knife. Cautiously, Chang stooped to pick up his knife, but he was nearly knocked off his feet as the Indian lunged. Chang quickly recovered his balance and immediately dropped into a fighting stance. Yellow Feather rapidly shifted his weight from one foot to the other as he made short thrusts at Chang first with his tomahawk then with his knife. Chang stayed just out of range of the violent onslaught. Chang tossed his knife to the ground and went into an arm-spread crouch, mimicking the movements Yellow Feather, minus a weapon.

Yellow Feather, pivoted his body to the left to better swing his tomahawk. Chang did likewise. As Yellow Feather feinted forward, Chang made a corresponding move backward. For several minutes, they stepped in unison, as if engaged in a pernicious dance. Laughter flared amid the crowd at the strange spectacle before them. Yellow Feather leapt at Chang in a scream of rage while swinging both weapons wildly. Chang easily sidestepped the intended blows. The crowd seemed fascinated with Chang and his unorthodox tactics. Yellow Feather continued swinging and jabbing his weapons at Chang, but was unable to connect with a single blow. With the speed of a striking snake, Chang grabbed Yellow Feather's arm as he rushed past. With short twist, Chang drove the Indian to the ground. The aborigine landed facedown in the dirt as both weapons tumbled from his grasp.

Struggling back to his feet, his face flushed with anger, Yellow Feather, charged like an angry bull. With long arms splayed and eyes seething with fury, the Indian rushed his small yellow tormentor once more. Bending low, he grabbed frantically at Chang who deftly stepped out of reach. As Yellow Feather hurtled by, Chang kicked the Indian's backside, sending him floundering into the crowd. The crowd was in a dither with laughter, so amused were they with the battle. With a little help from the bystanders, the warrior returned to the battle. He stumbled toward Chang who sent his opponent flying into the assemblage on the opposite side. Yellow Feather shook his head groggily, and staggered toward Chang. The Chinese soldier made the mistake of turning his head to smile at Zeb. At that moment, with an angry piercing yell, the Indian leapt at him. He caught Chang in a crushing bear hug that pinned arms to his sides. Yellow Feather's powerful grip made it difficult for Chang to breathe. Chang squirmed loose, aided by the slippery grease on his body. Yellow feather grabbed him again and Chang felt himself lifted from his feet as the Indian tried to squeeze the life out of him. Chang stiffened. Like a coiled spring, he kicked out in blinding speed, knocking the legs from under Yellow Feather. Both combatants sprawled on the ground.

Panting heavily, Chang regained his feet. As his opponent struggled to rise, Chang dropped him with a violent kick to the head. Yellow Feather lay beside the still-unconscious body of Claws that Walk. After prodding both Indians with his foot to ensure they were unconscious, Chang limped back to the fire where he sat beside Zeb. The women of the two defeated warriors ran to their men and helped them to their lodges. Chang's body glistened with sweat and grease. He turned toward Zeb and was about to speak when the captain fell in a rumpled heap on the ground. Blood oozed from a bullet wound on the back of his neck.

Three Fingers leapt across the fire to help Zeb lift Chang to a sitting position. The roaring crowd had apparently masked the crack of the rifle. Two other tribal elders quickly joined Three Fingers. They formed a shield around Chang to prevent the unknown would-be assassin from shooting him again. Chang looked around, but was unable to see the shooter. Zeb wiped away most of the blood. Chang reached up and felt the wound. The bullet had only grazed him just below his left ear. Zeb sighed in relief. Chang wasn't going to die. At least not today—not from this wound.

The chief ripped off one of his sleeves, handing the soft leather cloth to Zeb who tied it around Chang's neck to staunch the flow of blood. The other two chiefs stood. After much threatening and shouting, they disbursed the milling crowd. With order restored, the chiefs commanded their warriors to find the person who shot their guest Yellow Chief. Three Fingers turned to Chang and said, "You beat two of my finest warriors Yellow Chief. You will now lodge here as becomes a chief." Three Chiefs returned to his lodge, trailed by his woman.

As Zeb and Chang stood wondering what to do, five women dragged lodge poles and pre-formed animal hides to piece of flat ground near Three Fingers' lodge. Soon afterward, they erected a conical shaped lodge. As Chang looked on, Zeb said, "It's called a teepee. It's kind of a portable house. These nomadic plains Indians swear by them."

They had just completed staking the bottom of the lodge down when several boys led Zeb's packhorse to him. Zeb removed the pack and tossed it into the lodge saying, "Well, at least we know where we're going to sleep. It's a great honor for us to bed down near their chiefs. I ain't never been invited before. I think your neck is going to be stiff and sore for a few days, but unless your wound festers up I think you will be okay."

"I feel fine now, but if that shooter had been a little better shot all my problems here would be over. Did you see who took that pot-shot at me?"

"Nope. It might have been anyone, man, woman or child."

Early the next morning a young boy awakened Zeb and Chang, and told them to meet with the tribal elders. As soon as Chang and Zeb sat, Chief Three Fingers plucked a glowing ember from the fire to light a long-stemmed pipe. He took a few puffs and blew smoke to the north, south, east and west then he handed the pipe to Chang. Zeb explained they were showing their reverence to the four directions of mother earth. Chang followed their example then handed the pipe to Zeb, who repeated the ritual and passed the pipe back to one of the other elders who did likewise.

"Well," Zeb said, "They must accept you as a chief or they wouldn't have gave you the pipe. Only chiefs and great warriors can smoke it. Don't know why they included me in this ceremony."

Chief Three Fingers looked at Chang and said, "Yellow Chief, you are free to stay or go but some of my braves say that Claws that Walk slipped and fell. They say you did not defeat him. It does not matter what they say, we saw that you could have easily taken his scalp. His woman will bring you the scalp taken by Claws that Walk. The woman of Yellow Feather will do the same. Our warrior Bent Gun says he will fight you for the scalp he owns if you dare fight him. You decide."

Chang stated, "I will fight the warrior, but he will save himself great injury if he gives the scalp to me now."

—   —   —

An hour later, Chang walked unaccompanied through the village. As he did, he sensed a change of attitude toward him. The people seemed frightened. The women clubbed their dogs away from him and kept their children at a distance as he passed. He wondered if these people were much different from himself and his compatriots, or anyone else in the world for that matter. They all seemed to love their families. They cared and provided for them just like people everywhere. So absorbed in his thoughts was he that he didn't notice Zeb approach until he petulantly asked, "Are you crazy walking around out here alone? You done been shot once already."

"Everybody seems courteous to me. No one has caused me any trouble."

"Chang don't be a dang fool, the only reason they ain't pestering you is because they's afraid you'll stomp 'em, but that don't mean that some young buck mightn't back shoot you between the eyes. Besides that, you don't need to fight nobody else. You got the respect of the whole tribe now, even the ones what wants to kill you. This next Injun wants to fight you with a spear on horseback. He grew up with a spear in his hands. Why don't you back away from the fight? Take the scalps you won and get out of this camp or sure as shooting one of 'em is going to kill you sooner or later. What's it all fer anyway? It's just a little hair. Is that worth losing your life fer?"

"How does an Indian warrior like Bent Gun, use a spear? Will he throw it from horseback or try to ride close enough to thrust it through me? Will they provide me with a warhorse?"

"Does that make much difference?"

"Most certainly. A warhorse will react much differently in a battle than a nag."

"Sounds like you know a little about 'em," Zeb told Chang. "I ain't never seen a spear leave an Injun's hand until he is certain of a kill. They don't want to leave theirselves defenseless."

"That makes sense."

"And an Injun's horse is trained from the time it is weaned for no purpose but war and hunting. The most valuable possession a warrior owns is his warhorse. From what I seen, they ain't no better horsemen anywheres."

At the outer edge of the village, a small group of boys practiced shooting bows and arrows at a small log suspended by a braided rawhide rope from a tree limb. Zeb and Chang stopped to watch and Chang said, "I see they make a good horse bow, short and stout. Do they make and use a long siege bow also?"

"Not that I seen."

"Is the chief like a general in a battle?"

"Not exactly. Injuns rarely fight an organized war. They usually sneak up on their enemy with a small war party like they done to your people. They kill 'em and run. A warrior is free to join a war party, but he is also free to quit anytime it suits him. Boredom, hunger, rain—any of 'em is a good enough excuse to stop fighting and go home. That's why the Injuns usually lose battles to the United States Army. The army obeys orders and the Injuns don't. Injuns hardly ever fight together except when their village is threatened or attacked—then they're a different breed of cat. That is when the Injun does what the war chief tells him. It would take a mighty big army to attack and take this village. With that big a threat they'd up and move somewheres else."

—   —   —

The next morning the drums again began their incessant beat. Bent Gun pranced back and forth on his warhorse. He wore only a breechcloth around his waist. Noting the Indian's garb, Zeb asked Chang, "Why do you got all your clothes on now when you were stripped to the waist for yesterday's battle?"

"When fighting from horses it is better to be well-covered for added protection."

Zeb seemed puzzled. "Seems to me you ought to be protected when you're fighting on foot too. You don't make no sense at all."

A wall of warriors surrounded the battleground as Bent Gun waved his spear above his head. The war paint applied to the warrior and horse alike made them appear ferocious. A warrior led a small spotted pony to Chang. It had only a single woven leather rope looped around its neck. Zeb explained, "The rope is to lead him. You ride bareback with no reins. You probably ain't never fought no battle like this before. I think you should back out while you got the chance. This young buck has been riding bareback since he was knee high to a worm. If you was to quit right now you might still leave here with your hair still intact."

"I can't do that Zeb."

"I didn't figure you would, but you still ought to."

Chief Three Fingers handed Captain Chang a long slender wooden shaft tipped with a sharp iron spear point, and said, "This is my spear. I killed many buffalo and defeated many enemies with it." Then the chief turned and faced the battlefield as he sat by the elders.

Bent Gun galloped his horse across the field to show off his horsemanship. First, he dropped on one side of the horse's flanks, then the other. He spun himself around and rode backward, and once stood on the horse's back. He ended his wild performance with the horse bending its rear legs and sliding to a stop in front of the elders. The warrior leapt from his sweating, foam-flecked horse and landed lightly on his feet. The elders nodded their approval. Grinning broadly, Bent Gun turned to acknowledge the deafening shouts of the crowd, cheering his remarkable display.

Chang strode to the small spotted horse and removed the rope from its neck. He talked in its ear as he patted it its cheek. Grasping a handful of hair on the horse's mane, Chang effortlessly leapt astride its back. The pony trotted briskly to the arena as Chang controlled its sharp turns, stops, and acceleration with only knee pressure on its neck. When he was satisfied with the pony's performance, Chang stopped near the fire pit and alit on the ground next to Bent Gun. Chang noticed that the Indian warrior's horse was still breathing heavily, steam rising from its back. The two men faced Three Fingers and the tribal elders.

Bent Gun held his spear in hand as he remounted his horse. Holding the spear mid-shaft with his right hand, Bent Gun kicked the flanks of his horse, which responded haltingly before trotting to the far end of the arena. Chang stood holding his pony with one hand. He sprang to the back of the pony and maneuvered it to face the Indian warrior.

Bent Gun positioned himself low on the right side of the horse. Blurting a loud war cry, Bent Gun kicked his horse in the flanks to urge it forward into battle. It galloped toward Chang, somewhat more slowly than it had while Bent Gun was performing his equestrian act for the tribe. Chang was awaiting the maneuver. When it happened, Chang also charged forward. He knew his pony was fresher than the other horse and would respond to his commands more quickly. As they drew near to each other, Bent Gun hurled his sharp spear at Chang's mid-section. A moment before being impaled, Chang pivoted his horse to the right. Simultaneously, he swung his spear like a club and knocked the charging Indian from his horse. Chang slid from the pony and approached the warrior who regained his feet with some difficulty. Chang touched the warrior's chest with the tip of the spear.

Bent Gun stood proudly with chest out. He began singing. Chang assumed it was a death chant. He admired the young warrior's courage in the face of sure death. Chang gave a nod of approval, lowered the spear and remounted the pony. The horse cantered to the far end of the arena. While Chang's back was turned, Bent Gun retrieved his spear. The warrior caught his horse, jumped on its back and again charged Chang.

Chang faced away, apparently unaware that Bent Gun was about to skewer him. Just as Bent Gun came within striking distance, Chang swerved aside and the warrior thundered past, his spear tip missing Chang by a foot. As Chang turned, Bent Gun bore down on him again. Chang threw himself from his pony, as the spear narrowly missed him. The captain stumbled as he hit the ground, causing him to lose his grip on the spear. He popped to his feet when he heard Bent Gun's horse returning. He had no time to retrieve the spear.

Knowing the Indian's horse was nearly played out, Chang stood his ground. At the last second he stepped to the horse's left side, away from the deadly spear which Bent Gun held in his right hand. He grabbed the Indian's foot and heaved with such force that warrior and horse alike sprawled on the ground. The Indian's spear was driven into the dirt. The warrior quickly rolled over and stood up. He grabbed his spear and jerked it violently, breaking the tip off and leaving part of the jagged shaft protruding from the dirt. Bent Gun flung the broken portion of the shaft he held in his hand at Chang. The captain knocked the shaft away easily with the side of his hand. Bent Gun grabbed the spear that Chang had dropped just as Chang grabbed his pony's mane and pulled himself astride the horse. The warrior ran screaming toward Chang with upraised spear. Chang's pony pranced from side to side as Chang anticipated the warrior's attack. The pony shied away as Bent Gun neared, exposing Chang's left side to attack. Bent Gun seized the opportunity, and cast the spear with all his might. In desperation, Chang kicked the pony's flanks horse to flee, but the spear grazed his leg and embedded itself in the pony's side.

In a shriek of pain, the wounded animal leaped straight up, unseating Chang. He slammed the ground face first as the pony plunged into the crowd of bystanders, injuring several of them in the process. The crazed horse, spear still protruding from his side, swiveled and returned to the battle arena and trampled Chang who was still on the ground. Bent Gun retreated from the wounded animal as the pain-crazed horse, ignoring everything, charged the running Indian. Bent Gun turned to face the pony, which reared up and knocked the warrior to the ground with its front hooves. The Indian fell on his back just as a gunshot rang out, dropping the pony where it stood. Chang lay where the pony had trampled him as blood oozed from his body. He raised his head, and saw blood gushing from Bent Gun's abdomen. The warrior had fallen on precisely the spot where he had broken the tip of the spear in the ground. The jagged wooden shaft now spiked the Indian, pinning him to the ground.

Bent Gun's woman broke through the crowd and ran to the warrior. Another warrior eased the wailing woman away while others surrounded the inert body. The Indians made no attempt to remove the broken shaft from Bent Gun's body. Instead, they picked him up, shaft, spear tip and all, and carried him to his lodge. Zeb ran to assist Chang. Zeb asked for assistance, but received none. Zeb dragged Chang into their lodge. Backing through the entrance, Zeb laid Chang on a sleeping robe, wet down Chang's shirt and washed the blood and dirt from his body.

Chang was badly skinned and bruised, but apparently had no broken bones. A shallow laceration split his forehead, and it was plain that a monstrous bruise would soon appear. Several other minor scratches and lacerations were already clotting over. Chang's eyes cracked open. He tried to raise himself up, but Zeb held him down and said, "Take it easy there pardner. You're going to be okay. Probably be a mite sore for a few days, but I suspect you're plumb lucky to still be alive."

A few minutes later Chang heard agitate voices outside. He looked through the open flap of the entrance and saw a large group of warriors dressed in colorfully beaded buckskins. Most had one or more feathers in their hair, some pointed down and some pointed up. The chief and two other tribal elders wore a long feathered headdress hanging nearly to the ground. Zeb said, "Them varmints is having a real full-dress powwow. Them feathers is a badge of rank. This here group represents the top of the pecking order. I think, my friend, we are in a heap of trouble."

They watched as frenzied gestures and foot stomping spread through the group. After several minutes, it was obvious that no agreement had yet been reached. Chang grew weary and dozed off. When he awoke, the sun was down. Warriors still surrounded the fire pit, but the voices were no longer boisterous. Chief Three Fingers said something then returned to his lodge.

Zeb told Chang, "You may not be death personified, but you could sure be his second cousin. That pony done a pretty good job of stomping you out there. I can't believe your head ain't caved in."

Chang rubbed his head. "Are you sure it's not? It feels like it is. Zeb, I can't fight every day. There must be some way I can convince them to return the scalps."

"I've been thinking on that some," Zeb replied, "and the only way I can figure you could do it was if you could convince their squaws to make 'em give 'em back to you.

"These Injuns is deeply superstitious. They believe that a great spirit causes everything that happens in their lives. It's like a spirit of nature abiding in trees, mountains, birds or buffalo. They pray to this spirit to give 'em good luck in hunting, harvesting or hitching up with a wife. Even when they die it's some spirit what gets the blame. You could play on their superstitions by prowling around camp and causing a little ruckus. Like stampeding a few horses, setting fire to a lodge or two, or disrupting their food supply by chasing off the game. Pretty much anything that makes 'em uncomfortable scares 'em. Might not be long before the squaws would pressure the warriors into giving them scalps back to appease the big spirit.

"Problem is, there is just too many ifs. If you could get out of this Blackfoot camp alive; if you could get to Bannack or Virginia City alive; if you could learn to hide your tracks without the injuns finding 'em; if you could spot signs of Blackfoot warriors out hunting you. Nope, just too danged many ifs. To tell you the truth, I don't know what you should do."

"You have shown me the skill these Blackfoot have to track people and animals. Are there any Indians better at tracking than the Blackfoot?"

"Well, there is the Nez Perce tribe. You can find them about a hundred miles north of Bannack and Virginia City. The Nez Perce, is the very best there ever was. They scare the hell out of these here Blackfoot 'cause they never know when the Nez Perce is around camp till after the horses is stolen. They ain't no love lost between 'em. The Nez Perce is pretty good folks as far as Injuns go. They are mostly peaceful. Real friendly to us white folks. They is famous fer raising horses, especially a little black and white pony they call an appaloosa. This breed of horse is the smartest there ever was. You was just riding one of 'em with Bent Gun. Injuns from all over the country, and even down in Mexico, come to trade for 'em. The Nez Perce ain't no slouch when it comes to horse trading, or horse stealing for that matter.

"The Nez Perce is clever. They keep fooling these here Blackfoot into raising some of their horses for 'em. Every year, the Blackfoot send out a horse stealing party and steals some Nez Perce horses nice and easy like. The Nez Perce lets 'em keep them horses grazing and training 'em. Then, just before the snow falls, the Nez Perce comes and steals 'em back. Happens every year, and the Blackfoot still thinks they are getting the best of the deal. They thinks they're out-stealing the Nez Perce. But there ain't no way you can get from here to the Perce Nez without getting yourself killed, so it's best you forget about it."

Chief Three Fingers entered the lodge and said, "I will tell you what my people say, so hear me well. My people know the ways of the white man when he trades with us. What he can't trade he steals. Some white men shoot us only to see if we will die. That is the way of the white man. My people also know the ways of the yellow man. He is the squaw of the white man. He does for them what they will not do for themselves. He cleans their lodges and washes their clothes. He cooks for them, and tries to find the yellow metal in the water after the white man leaves.

"The yellow man does not fight the white man, he does not fight the red man. The yellow man is the squaw of the white man. Many of my warriors want to give you to their women to do with you as they please. I will not let this happen to the Yellow Chief who has shown us he is a brave warrior. The council decided that Yellow Chief must return to the white man's camp where they harvest the yellow metal. Go and rejoin your people. Tell your yellow brothers never to enter Blackfoot country looking for the yellow metal. If they do, we will cut off their scalps as we did those of your brothers. It would be wise for you to leave our village soon. If Bent Gun dies from his wound I cannot protect you from his squaws and brothers."

Chang arose stiffly and said, "I value your words as I do the words of Shoots Long Shots. I will leave your camp shortly and after I have gone tell your people that the warrior they know as Yellow Chief will make war against the Blackfoot until they give me the scalps of my brothers. Until then I will only speak to the Blackfoot with my weapons."

Three Fingers stared in amazement at the arrogance of Chang's words. A smile stole across the chief's face as he removed the headdress from his head and placed it on Chang's. The chief then stalked out of the lodge.

Zeb let out a long sigh and said, "Chang, you damn fool, you talked yourself into your grave this time. The chief won't say nothing till you're long gone, but when he does every Injun in camp is going to be coming after your scalp. I think you best get you a horse and skeedaddle on back up to Bannack or Virginia City."

"I meant what I said Zeb. If I have to I'll fight the whole Blackfoot tribe until they return the scalps of my people." More softly he said, "But I'd rather not."

"Now you stay put while I go out and see what's going on," Zeb told Chang as he ducked through the entrance flap. A few minutes later Zeb returned and said, "I ain't never seen Injuns as stirred up as these varmints is. If Bent Gun dies, which looks likely, they will turn you over to their squaws fer sure. If that happens I'll put a bullet into you myself. They'd tie you to a pole and skin you alive. Then they'd put you on a spit over the fire for a little slow roasting. I figure once you're out of camp every warrior here will try to be the first to catch you. If I was you, which I ain't, but if I was, and I was any good at running, I would borrow that Hawkins rifle of mine over there and the pistol I got in my pack, and slip out of this camp real quiet like. And I'd do it right quick."

"Thank you," said Chang.

"And if I was you," Zeb continued, "I'd stick to rough, rocky ground to make it tough for tracking and for horses. Oh, they can still follow your tracks, but with you having my guns they ain't going to want to get within rifle range of you. And if I was running for my life on foot, like you is, I would have to figure on what was the easiest and fastest way to get to the white man's gold diggings. I'd also be sure if I was you, not to go that way 'cause that's the way they'll figure you'll go. You can bet these Injuns will have every trail watched by some of their young'uns who want to get their warrior status. They'll spot you, an use smoke signals to tell the others where you is.

"And lastly, if I was you, I would take it kind of easy, conserve my strength, hide out, and pick one or two off with my rifle on occasion. You know, keep 'em off balance. That way I'd be setting the pace, and running the show, even when they think they is."

Scribing the dirt with the tip of his knife, Zeb drew a rough map, "This here is how you get to the gold diggings, but like I says, don't go straight there. You'll have to outthink 'em and take a more roundabout route." Pointing to his pack, he said, "Might be something else in there you could use, but remember you're going to be loaded pretty heavy lugging my rifle and pistol. So don't take nothing that'll bog you down, and remember, Injuns don't fight at night if they can help it. They figure if they gets killed in the dark they can't find their way to the Happy Hunting Grounds."

"But they killed my countrymen at night," Chang protested.

"I don't guess they thought that was a fight. They was just slaughtering 'em, everyone asleep and all. Another thing, don't never get yourself boxed in. If you hole up somewhere, make sure you've got a way out. If they get you cornered, you're a goner. Now mine you take good care of my rifle. It's hand built. A Hawkins shoots plumb straight near far as you can see. On the other hand, that there revolver makes a lot of smoke and noise and scares the hell out of people, but it ain't like a rifle. Don't expect to hit nothing over fifty feet, and even under fifty feet you'll probably miss half of what you're shooting at. I'm going to go snoop around again. If I don't see you when I get back you take care of yourself. I got to confess that I ain't doing all this just 'cause I like you. I figure as long as the Blackfoot are busy chasing you they won't go on the warpath against my people traveling the immigrant road."

As Zeb started out the entrance Chang stood, shook Zebs hand and said, "I have put you into a very tough spot Zeb, but thanks for your help. I'll try to take good care of your rifle and handgun, but I ain't promising nothing." Chang said the last part of the sentence in mock imitation of Zeb's accent."

Zeb laughed. "So long my friend," he said before making his exit. After Zeb left the lodge, Chang limped to the rifle. Removing it from its leather case, he looked it over. It had a long metal ramrod positioned below the barrel. A new percussion cap nipple was screwed tightly into the base of the barrel where the original flint and steel powder ignition mechanism had once been. From his military training, he knew that this simple device, the so-called nipple, when fitted with a percussion cap, made this gun a reliable all-weather weapon. Its long rifled barrel made it extremely accurate at long range.

Chang leaned the rifle against the wall and picked up a bag. Zeb called it his possible bag. It was made of leather and contained everything he needed to load a rifle or pistol—gunpowder, percussion caps, greased bullet patches and lead cast bullets. The gunpowder was in a hard-shelled, watertight container, and the powder flask had a small metal spout formed at the top with a small lever built in. By inverting the powder flask and rotating the lever, it dumped a measured powder charge down the rifle barrel. Once that was done, the only other necessary steps to loading the rifle were to take a small leather patch wrapped around a lead bullet, ram it tightly against the powder and push a pre-formed percussion cap onto the nipple.

After ensuring the possible bag contained everything he needed, Chang set it near the rifle. Chang opened Zeb's pack. He rummaged through it until he found the pistol. He saw a couple of other useful items, and taking Zeb at his word, he decided to take them too. First, he removed a hip-length jacket with two large pockets, and slipped it on over his shirt. He also grabbed a handful of jerky. He put the jerky in one pocket and the pistol in the other. Scrounging further, he pocketed a telescope and donned a pair of thick buffalo-soled moccasins. He had been barefoot since the massacre of his people. It would be nice to have a little protection for his naked feet.

Looping the possible bag over his shoulder, Chang shouldered the rifle and stepped out of the lodge. There he noticed a couple of woven leather ropes lying coiled at its base. Not missing a stride, he leaned down and picked them up looping them over his head. He kept to the shadows as he headed for the river crossing and away from the Indian camp.

-FOUR-

NORTH AMERICA AUGUST 1862

MONTANA TERRITORY

BLACKFOOT COUNTRY

COMING TO THE shallow river, Captain Chang glanced back to see if anyone followed. He saw no one, so he waded across the stream and started up a steep slope toward the main trail above. Nearing the top, he checked again for any sign of pursuit. He heard no noise, and saw no movement. He kept his head turned toward the camp as he inched his way up the last few feet. He was nearly at the apex when he heard a horse snort. Reflexively, his hand went to the revolver in his jacket pocket. His head whipped around and he was startled to find himself looking up into the face of a single horse rider.

In the dark, Chang could not see the man's facial features, but neither of them said a word. After a few seconds, the rider urged his mount down the slope and across the river into the darkened Indian camp. He realized that the Indians must have been watching him from the moment he left the lodge. In hindsight, he remembered that no dogs snapped at his heels as they usually did. The women must have chased the dogs away from the only escape route. They are toying with me, he thought.

He could see nothing out of the ordinary in the village below. Countless campfires flickered, silhouetting the teepees. The dogs yapped, and he saw shadowy shapes of people as they passed near the fires. Knowing that Indians hated to fight in the dark, Chang thought he might avoid pursuit until daylight. He learned survival skills in the army. I will use those skills to survive, he thought. Standing on the trail where he could see the village, he practiced loading the rifle until he became proficient at it. With a last look at the Blackfoot village, he shifted his rifle to a comfortable angle and followed the trail toward the massacre site of his people. Traveling all night, he entered the mining camp just as the sun peeked over the hilltop. Getting a cold drink from the stream and sitting back for a breather, he choked up at seeing the remains of his murdered people still beside the fire pit. He wished he could return them to their families in China, but he didn't see how he could do that. Once he got help, what was left of the charred remains would crumble to dust aboard the ship en route to China.

The trail he followed earlier from Virginia City went north. The Indians would expect him to follow it back to the gold mining camp and ambush him along the way. Although he followed the trail all night, he decided that from now on he'd better follow Zeb's advice and keep to the roughest ground. He also needed to stay in the open so he could use the rifle to pick them off from long distance, and it would make it a little tougher for them to ambush him. He would have to give them at least a few surprises to show them it wouldn't be as easy to kill a lone Chinaman on as they expected. The soldier in him told him to keep to the high ground. That he would do. They expected him to go north to Virginia City, so he would go south towards the Fort Hall Trading Post. It was in the middle of Shoshone and Bannack country. Since they were on poor terms with the Blackfoot, they might even give him a little unintended protection of which they were unaware.

It was already getting hot. Chang gobbled down a couple of jerky strips, filled his water pouch and drank deeply from the stream. It might be some time before he reached water again. He turned north toward Virginia City, hoping to fool a few of his pursuers. About a mile up, he ducked off the trail and slowly angled west then south towards the foothills of a small mountain range rising in the distance.

He kept a brisk pace, keeping to the lowest slopes of the undulating sagebrush-covered plain, studded with volcanic mounds. He stopped for a breather as he scanned the trail behind. So far, he saw no sign of pursuit. Early in the afternoon, he arrived at a small butte. He cut up one side and climbed nearly to the top. Looking back at the path he had followed, he saw several puffs of smoke rising in the air. The smoke must be signaling his direction of travel.

He used the telescope to scan the trail and spotted two Indians on horseback right off. Their heads faced down as they followed his tracks. The two zigzagged, probably expecting his tracks to veer north again towards Bannack or Virginia City. Chang guessed that the two Indians were about two hours behind. He guessed he could make it to the mountains before they caught him, at least he would try. An hour later he stood at the base of the barrier. The mountain range rose abruptly from the flat desert floor. Numerous deep, rocky gullies and sharp ridges crisscrossed the lower slopes. Lava rock lay strewn about the area, a victim of eons of erosion. The rugged foothills rose half way up the mountain and butted into a vertical lava rock cliff raising several hundred feet. It appeared to be an impregnable wall. Unless he could scale that looming cliff, he might be trapped. He hadn't the time to scout the mountains so he decided to take the best position he could hold the Indians off until dark. Maybe he could slip away then.

He followed a deep gully to the vertical wall of the cliff. There he discovered he was on a narrow stone shelf. He had a clear view for several hundred yards in front and to the sides. He knew that cliff would prevent anyone from circling behind him. It was the best defensive position he was likely to find. He moved behind a boulder where he lay his rifle down. Beside it, he placed the rope and possible bag, and the pistol from his pocket.

Looking up the face of the cliff, he could see a few spots where he could possibly scale it. There were narrow crevices and splits in the lava rock wall for hand and foot holds, but it was too light to make the attempt now. The mounted warriors would spot him easily.

He espied the horsemen still following his track, and he estimated they would be in rifle range within the hour. He wondered why no other warriors had shown up yet, but he assumed others would be along shortly. He still ached from being trampled by the horse. The injuries, coupled with the lack of sleep and the rigorous escape, combined against him. As soon as he sat, he realized his fatigued body was ready to collapse. He needed rest, he needed sleep, but he dared not take the time for either. Instead, he got up and scouted the immediate area. Near the base of the cliff, he skirted a boulder and discovered a small cave hidden behind it. A small irregular tunnel marked the entrance to the cave. There was dark soot on the ceiling and figures scratched in the rock of the cave walls.

"An excellent shelter," he muttered, "But I would hate to be trapped in here. Just then, he noted a faint breeze and realized there must be another opening in the back of the cave to allow the airflow. He followed the breeze to the back of the cave. It grew darker but he could make out a pile of fallen rock. He held he hand next to the stones and felt cool air coming from between them. He felt around with his hand and discovered an opening just big enough for him. He crawled through the opening and it became lighter again. He looked up and discovered a narrow split in the rocks leading upward. Easily climbing the narrow gully, he exited above the cliff on a rather large flat area. It dropped straight down the cliff to the north and sloped gently to the plain below on the south.

Pleased he wasn't cornered, he retraced his steps to retrieve his weapons. He hunkered down behind the rocks to look for the Indian warriors. His parched mouth and throat felt as if they were about to seal shut. He grabbed the water pouch and discovered that it leaked. He finished off the last few drops of liquid and tossed the bag aside. His throat was sore from the dusty, dry trail and breathing was difficult. He wasn't sure if he was more tired or thirsty. Shrugging these problems aside, he watched the two warriors with the telescope. Although they continued on, their pace slowed. They kept looking in Chang's direction. He was certain they had not spotted him yet, but they apparently realized their vulnerability. They dismounted their horses and walked slowly, but still they approached.

Then the Indians stopped. One looked at the tracks and pointed in Chang's general direction. Then the Indians turned the warhorses loose. The horses did not go far, but immediately began grazing on the sparse desert grass. Then, resuming their pursuit, the Indians ascended the hill.

Chang figured they were now within rifle range. He stood and had one of the Indians in his gun sights, but could not pull the trigger. He knew their plans for him, but he simply could not shoot because they hadn't yet tried to kill him. Then one of the Indians gave a hand signal, and both dove for cover. They had spotted him, and were taking aim with their muskets. Chang ducked behind the boulder just as a bullet ricocheted from it.

Chang peeked around the boulder and saw the Indians scurrying from rock to rock. One made a hand signal to the other and they separated, one going left and the other right. Each hunkered down behind the cover of rocks and scrub bushes. After another hand signal, both Indians raised their muskets to their shoulders. Chang saw a puff of smoke erupt from the gun of the one on the left and almost simultaneously heard the smack of a bullet hitting the rocks behind him, followed by the report of the gun. Then smoke belched from the musket of the Indian on the right. An instant later Chang was momentarily blinded by fragments of rock kicked up directly in front of him.

The warrior on the left reloaded faster than Chang expected and was again ready to shoot. After the Indian fired, Chang saw the gunman's head remain in sight for a couple of seconds afterward, apparently to see where the bullet struck. Chang kept under cover of the boulder as the two warriors continued shooting at him. He also noted the time between seeing the smoke of the shooters' guns until he heard the bullet strike the rocks around him. He judged accurately when it was safe to raise his head between shots to see if the warriors had changed positions.

Chang was in no hurry to return fire. After all, he wasn't the only one with a limited supply of ammo. The more they shot, the less ammunition they had. Since the Indians shot at Chang several times and received no return fire, who knows what they were thinking. Perhaps they thought he did not know how to use a rifle, or that the rifle was faulty. At any rate, the Indians became less cautious. They began to stand higher and longer behind their cover after each shot.

As the standoff continued, Chang once came close to losing his life. He was slower than usual in ducking behind cover, and had barely pulled his head below the rock when he heard a whoosh. He felt a light breeze in his face as an arrow whizzed past his head to clatter in the rocks behind him. Chancing a quick look, Chang located the warrior that shot the arrow. Chang ducked down again. He was shaken by how narrowly the arrow missed his head. Summoning his courage, he cautiously raised himself and rested his rifle between two solid rocks.

He took careful aim at the position where he saw the warrior on his right raise his head. As if on cue, the Indian stood to shoot. Chang aimed at the smoke from the Indian's gun. The Chinese soldier squeezed the trigger and felt the recoil slam into his shoulder. The warrior jerked erect and stumbled backward, dropping his musket on the rocks ahead of him.

Chang dropped behind the boulder as he reloaded. When the rifle was ready to fire again, he peered between the rocks. Bringing the rifle up, he took aim at the last position where he had seen of the Indian on the left. Chang hoped the warrior hadn't changed locations. Chang was surprised to see the warrior stand to full height. Taking advantage of the foolish mistake, Chang aimed and fired. As the smoke cleared, he saw the Indian hurtle backward into the rocks and lay still.

Reloading, Chang set his sights on the position of the first warrior, uncertain as to whether he would pop up again. Wiping the sweat from his eyes, he continued scan the area.

The Indians' horses had not moved far from where they began grazing. Then at a distance, he saw a large group of horsemen riding toward him. He estimated that the whole bunch would be on him in less than an hour. He picked up the pistol and checked it for the 20th time to make sure it was loaded and ready to fire. He crept through the rocks toward the Indians he had shot. He remained vigilant, hoping that one of the Indians were not simply feigning injury to surprise him.

The second Indian he shot lay motionless on his back. Lifeless eyes stared at the sky, the hole in his neck doing likewise. Then Chang shifted his attention to the other warrior. With his pistol cocked and ready to shoot, Chang peeked over the rock where he had last seen the Indian. He was sprawled stiffly amid blood-splattered rocks. A dark round hole had bored through the head just above his right eye. Chang felt nauseous. He had snuffed out the lives of these two warriors. He tried to balm his conscience with the knowledge that they had shown him no mercy, but so far, the tactic wasn't working.

Chang pulled the powder and bullet bags from the necks of the two dead warriors. Next he collected their muskets and returned to his former position behind the boulder. As he looked through the Indians possible bags, he discovered they carried their powder in small clay bottles. One bag carried gunpowder and a smaller one contained priming powder. Large, heavy bullets lay loose in the bottom of the bag. Their firearms were of poor quality. They were simple flint and steel, smooth bore, large caliber trade muskets. They could not be very accurate at long range, but would be extremely lethal at close range.

There was at least an hour of daylight left. The warriors racing toward him were only minutes away, so he would never hold them all off until dark. He was going to have to make a break for it. Thinking he might need more gunpowder for his rifle, he poured some of the Indians gunpowder in his hand. It was coarse and lumpy—probably unreliable. He wasn't going to bet his life on it. However, it reminded him of an incident he had seen in China some years ago. Chi Ching was a newly appointed officer of the lowest rank. He was short and plump, and wore thick eyeglasses. He couldn't march, couldn't give orders and could rarely do anything without his squad of soldiers laughing at him. Although he was terrible soldier, he was a genius at improvising and setting up lethal trooper traps as he called them.

During a border clash with a neighboring warlord, Chang had seen Chi Ching set up small, concealed bombs triggered with a trip string. They were effective in blowing the legs off unwary soldiers. Chi Ching was equally talented at constructing other booby traps to maim and cripple his enemies.

Chang began at once to construct trooper traps from the Indians' guns and powder. He removed the flint from one gun to prevent it from firing as he filled the barrel with a mix of gunpowder and pebbles. When the barrel was full, he removed a limb from a nearby desert plant and forced it down the barrel, breaking it off at the muzzle. Satisfied that it would function as a bomb, he did the same to the other gun. He pulled a long strong thread from one of the sleeves of Zeb's jacket and set both guns on the boulder. He tied the thread around the triggers of the muskets and threaded it around some rocks. Anyone picking up either gun, or hitting the concealed thread with his foot would trigger the bombs. He carefully filled the primer pan of both guns and replaced the flints with the hammers in the cocked position. He then backed away from what he hoped would be a surprise to unwary warriors.

Chang finished making the bombs in time to see a score of Blackfoot warriors converging on him. Some were already within rifle range. Picking up his rifle, he carefully sighted on the lead Indian and squeezed the trigger. Chang thought his chance of hitting a moving target at this range, at least four hundred yards, was not good. He was surprised when the warrior's horse dropped in mid-stride and rolled head over heels, throwing its rider in a heap to be trampled by the horses racing up behind.

Chang said, "Zeb did not exaggerate the range and accuracy of his rifle." He quickly reloaded and watched the Indians dismount, fan out and creep up the slope. Each one zigzagged from rock to rock for cover, just as their two fellow warriors had done earlier. Hearing angry shouting, he figured the warriors must have discovered the bodies of their two fallen brothers. In apparent blind anger, the Indians charged up the slope.

Chang waited until the first of the oncoming warriors was close enough for a pistol shot. Chang took careful aim and fired a round. He was gratified to see the warrior fall backward and lay motionless on the ground. Chang chose his targets, taking out the closest and most threatening. He quickly triggered three more shots. The closest Indians hesitated then dove for cover. Eventually the whole bunch retreated out of pistol range in a panic.

During the confusion caused by Chang's sudden attack, he pocketed his pistol, picked up his rifle and retreated to the cave. He scurried out the back exit and through the gully to the flat plateau on top. He scooted along in a crouch, and crawled the last few feet to the lip of the cliff. He peered cautiously downward at the Blackfoot warriors who hunkered down behind rocks and anything they could hide behind to keep out of sight of the deadly yellow man.

Chang scooted away from the cliff face then turned and ran several hundred feet back from the cliff. He set his rifle aside gathered an armful of dry twigs and branches. After throwing them in a pile, he cut some green shrubs with his knife and added them to the pile. He poured the Indians' gunpowder into the center of the brush pile, and trailed the last bit of it to the side. He put a cap on the nipple of his empty pistol, cocked and fired it into the string of gunpowder, and watched it flare up to ignite the brush pile. A dense column of smoke spiraled skyward.

Chang pocketed the pistol and picked up his rifle. He took one last look at the smoky fire and sprinted down the steep south slope of the mountain. He approached a thin dark ribbon of scrubby trees snaking through the plain below. He hoped the trees marked to path of a stream. He needed for water. Without it, his mind would soon become addled. He set his course to intersect the stream at the closest point, if it was a stream. His pace slowed as the night deepened. It wouldn't do to sprain an ankle or break a leg.

He hoped he had created a fair amount of confusion among the Indians with his smoky fire. If he were lucky, they would think the Shoshone or Bannack tribes started the fire. He began to wonder if the Blackfoot warriors had discovered the trap he laid. His answer came at once when a faint double boom echoed across the desert floor.

Chang guessed that at least two warriors would be occupied taking the bodies of their fallen brothers back to their village. He also assumed that when they discovered Chang was gone they knew there was no way over the mountain by horseback, so they would have to ride many miles to reach the other side of the mountain. From there they would again have to find Chang's tracks before they would know for sure in which direction he was heading. All these factors would create some confusion among the Indians, and would surely slow them down.

Well after midnight, Chang arrived at valley floor. He was grateful to see a shallow stream running there. He began to wonder if the stream would dry up because he drank so much water. He checked his firearms and was shocked to see that the pistol was empty. He had forgotten to reload it. Such lapses of memory could kill him, and he couldn't let it happen again. He sat down to rest, and before he knew it, he was asleep on the ground. A couple of hours later an animal's cry startled him awake. His body protested when he jerked upright. His head pounded, but he knew he had to start moving again. He took another draught of water and followed the creek. Best keep near a water supply, he thought. At dawn he stumbled from fatigue. He needed more sleep badly.

Noticing a cinder cone rising abruptly from the desert floor about a hundred yards west of the creek, he veered toward it. From atop it, he would have a good view of the surrounding area. He climbed to the summit and looked around. There was no sign of pursuit, so after loading and laying his weapons within easy reach, he scrunched his body into the rocks and was asleep within seconds. When he awoke at last is was already nearly sundown. He lay quietly listening to a faint noise coming, he thought, from the north. Easing himself to his knees, and keeping well below the tops of the rocks surrounding him, he peered through a gap between two rocks. His heart sank when he saw a large group of Indians riding directly toward him less than a mile away. He was confused as to why they were coming from the north when the warriors he had battled were to the south.

He looked about but saw no smoke signals. Perhaps these were Shoshone, but if they weren't he was afraid there may be no escape this time. He studied them through his telescope and finally determined from the war paint and dress that this was a Blackfoot war party. He counted seven warriors, all of whom boasted black, white and yellow zigzagging slashes of vivid war paint across their faces and torso. Similar patterns were painted on the heads and chests of their horses. All but one were armed with bows and arrows slung across their backs. Several also carried long spears. One, however, carried a rifle across his thighs. The warrior with the gun was also the only one with feathers in his hair. He had shoulder-length braids and appeared to be older than the others were. Chang remained out of sight as the war party approached. None of the riders made any indication that they were aware of Chang's presence. The captain held his breath as they dismounted beside the creek. They were well within range of both his rifle and pistol. The warriors pulled their riding blankets from their horses. Now Chang knew they were unaware of his presence.

One of the warriors led the horses up creek to a small grassy area where they were loosed. The Indians built a small smokeless fire and put two rabbits on to roast. After they ate, boisterous horseplay began. These were young warriors, probably on their first war party. The older Indian was likely more experienced.

Chang chuckled to himself as he watched the young men frolic. They looked to be in there teens. They yelled, laughed, wrestled and raced until just before dark. Then the older warrior stood and yelled at them as he gestured with his arms. The horseplay stopped abruptly, and each warrior wrapped himself in a blanket. They prostrated themselves, head to toe, in a circle around the fire. After the young warriors bedded down, the older one turned and strode straight toward Chang.

The Indian climbed nearly to the top of the hill. Chang, with knife in hand, waited to slit his throat if he came any closer. However, just short of the summit, the warrior leader looked over the area for a few minutes before returning to camp. He then walked toward the horses where he wrapped himself in his blanket and leaned back against some rocks. He was guarding the horses.

Chang waited until the campfire flickered out before silently gathering his weapons and supplies, and creeping down the slope toward the horses. As he neared them, the Indian was still lying back, wrapped in his blanket. Crouching down, Chang crept toward the warrior. When Chang was within a few feet, one of the horses whinnied. The Indian awoke with a start. Chang immediately leapt forward. Swinging his pistol viciously, Chang struck the warrior just above his ear, crushing his skull and killing him instantly.

Chang looked at the young warriors on the ground. None stirred. The Chinese soldier approached the skittish horses, gathered all seven lead ropes and led them as quietly as possible up creek until he was out of earshot of the Indian camp. He then mounted one of the horses. While retaining the lead ropes of the others, he rode north across the desert.

Several miles from the camp, Chang drew his pistol and put the barrel to the head of one of the horses and shot. He did not want the Indians to retried their horses and come after him. The horse crumpled to the ground. The other horses were used to hearing gunshots so they merely flinched slightly at the crack of the pistol. They continued following obediently. After shooting four more horses, Chang was able to increase his pace since he now only had one horse to lead. He knew he was pushing the horse he rode too hard from its foaming nostrils, sweat-soaked hide and labored breathing. It gone about as far as it was capable of going. He pulled the other horse alongside, and without dismounting, he jumped to the back of the other horse. He released the horse he had been riding. He did not shoot the horse this time, figuring he was too far away from his pursuers for them to find it. Eventually some lucky Indian or prospector would likely find the fine stray horse.

Chang's horse climbed for a couple of hours through a steep-walled canyon winding through a forest of tall aspens. When they eventually gave way to evergreen pines, he knew he was nearing the top of the mountain. He gained the summit of a ridge shortly after dawn. He dismounted the tired horse and from the top of the ridge, he viewed the canyon he just passed through. He saw no sign that anyone followed.

When he saw how far he had traveled during the night he realized what a godsend the horses had been.

He hid the horse in the trees. Using one of the long leather ropes, he tied it in a grassy area where it could feed. He figured he could turn the well-trained warhorse loose and it wouldn't stray far, but he didn't want to chance it. A bear or mountain lion could spook it, and Chang was too tired to give chase.

He leaned against a fallen tree where he could overlook the valley below. He was more exhausted than he thought, because his eyes nearly slammed shut. His last thought before nodding off was that he might receive a Blackfoot arrow or musket ball in his head at any time.

Chang slept the day away. It was nearly sundown when he arose. He scanned the valley with the telescope and saw no movement below. He retrieved the rested horse, but neither of them had a drop of water in perhaps 18 hours. Nevertheless, Chang felt more refreshed than he had in many days. He hoped the horse felt as well.

Chang rode the horse while there was still sufficient light, but clouds moved in after sundown and it grew too dark to see the path so he dismounted. He didn't want the horse to stumble and break a leg. Faint lights twinkled in the distance. It must be the gold mining town of Bannack. There he would have sanctuary in the Chinese tong house.

The terrain flattened as he entered the foothills. There clouds parted and the moons shown through, giving the horse light to see by. Chang remounted and the pace quickened. He was now in the rugged, rolling hills of Horse Prairie, part of a larger area known as Big Hole Basin. Aptly named, the deep basin featured gentle rolling hills covered with sagebrush and greasewood. Occasionally, a deep gully appeared where a stream had eroded the land. Grasshopper Creek was similar to the other streams cutting a channel through the hills, except that it had more free milling gold. Free milling meant that stream had milled the gold out of the rocks, depositing the pure metal in the bed over eons.

Grasshopper Creek, so named for the hoards of pesky insects infesting the area when the first prospectors discovered the stream, flowed through a highly mineralized geological formation. The formation began deep in the earth before volcanic pressure forced it to the surface. The flowing stream broke up the gold-rich rock then the heavy gold metal sank to the bottom as the lighter material washed downstream. Grasshopper

Creek snaked down out of the foothills through a deep-walled canyon then turned through a flatland where the gold mining town of Bannack sprang up seemingly overnight.

Chang rode the outskirts of Bannack. It looked like it had doubled in size in just the short time he had been away. Hundreds of tents, rough lumber buildings, and dugouts lined the northern bank of the creek and half way up a steep hill to the west. There were new buildings, including several miners' supply businesses, a new café and a blacksmith with a stable. Even a large two-story hotel gleamed in the moonlight.

The town was mostly dark, although a few lanterns shone here and there. It was relatively quiet as he rode up a small hill toward a large wooden building located at the far western edge of town. The building was black as pitch. No lights shone anywhere in it. He dismounted the horse and led it into a barn at the rear of the building. After watering and feeding the horse, Chang took rifle in hand and climbed the few steps to the back door of the tong house.

-FIVE-

North America   September 1862
Montana Territory
Bannack

The Bannack tong house, constructed by Chinese labor from hand-sawn lumber the previous winter, was located atop a knoll. The town was the first and largest settlement in the new territory of Montana. The building was unique in that it was the only completely painted structure in town, perhaps in the whole territory. Its high pointed roofline bespoke typical Oriental architecture. Upswept, graceful curves connected daintily with hand-carved eaves. The gables, eaves and window shutters were a bright garish purple, a sharp contrast to the rest of the pure, white structure.

The tong house was central to the Chinese community. It functioned as the focal point of community affairs and office of the current tong. It served as Chinese courthouse, jail and anything else needed. To the rest of the local population, the tong house was known as the joy house. The Chinese never joined their neighbors for a drink of good American whiskey. Many of the white Americans thought the tong house was a vice center. Whites thought it served as an opium den, a whorehouse and a gambling hall, but the Chinese in the tong house never used opium and other drugs.

The Chinese population laughed at the concept the white men had of their community center, but they did all they could to foster this belief. It kept many curious people away. The resident tong had impeccable character. He hired on specifically to administer every phase of the gold operations in Bannack. His dealings were fair and impartial. He negotiated with the white man to buy or lease gold mines in the area, and he provided plenty of laborers to local gold mining and construction projects.

Laborers came from sponsors in China. The sponsors paid the workers' travel expenses, but once they arrived in America the tong assumed full responsibility for them. He assigned work locations, and helped them find lodging and food. Essentially, they became his people. He attempted to ensure fair and impartial treatment for his people. All had equal opportunity to work the richer mines or higher-paid construction jobs. The working arrangement proved to be very profitable to everyone involved—the sponsors, the workers, and the administrators. The tong was, for the Chinese, essentially a territorial governor. His word was law. He was judge and jury. There was no appeal to his sentencing. He could impose a fine, banish the offender from the territory or even perform an execution.

The top floor of the tong house was a single large room. At night, it served as a dormitory for transient Chinese laborers as they waited for work assignments. During the day, it was a recreational center. A pile of sleeping mats and blankets dominated one corner. Anyone needing a place to sleep grabbed a mat and blanket and bedded down in any free space available. The lower floor had a huge kitchen toward the rear. The remainder of the lower floor served as an office. Several long tables stood near the front door. The tong worked at a huge desk in the center of the room where he kept his official records and correspondence. Chang stayed at this tong house before and knew the layout of the building. He entered through the rear door, walked through the kitchen and went upstairs to the dormitory. He pulled out a mat and immediately fell asleep. At last, he felt safe.

Well after daylight, a manservant awakened Chang. The servant said, "Breakfast is in the kitchen. After you eat, the tong would like to see you in his office."

While he ate, Chang considered the best way to report the massacre of his people. After the meal, he went to the tong's office. Tong Zing Yong sat at his desk thumbing through papers. When he saw Chang he said, "Captain Chang, it's so good to see you. Please tell me how our people are doing at the stream in the south. "Do I need to send more people there to help?" Tong Zing Yong was a short, heavy, middle-aged man with a round face. A wide pleasant smile and a twinkle in his intense black eyes bespoke good humor. He leaned back in his chair and motioned Chang to sit in a chair opposite the desk.

Chang paused momentarily then said, "Honorable Tong Zing Yong, I have bad news. All of our people there are dead."

Zing Young bolted upright, the smile replaced by consternation. "Dead? All ten of them? Are you sure Captain?"

"Yes sir, I'm sure. The only reason I'm still alive is due to the help of a white man. He found me buried in the mud."

Zing Yong shook his head. "I fear this occurred because of my error of judgment. I should never have sent them there unprotected, but I'm grateful you survived. If I ever find this man who saved your life perhaps I can reward him for helping you." After a few seconds of silence the tong continued, "Captain, I'm told you rode in on a little horse like those used by the Indians. Where did you get it?"

Chang told the tong of his experiences in the Blackfoot camp, and his attempt to recover the scalps of the slain Chinese. Yong's face hardened, his eyes boring into Chang's. Then the tong's emotions erupted. He pounded his fist on the desktop and stood so abruptly the chair overturned backward and slid ten feet across the floor. He jerked open a wooden cabinet, rummaged through it and with a grunt removed several pages. He righted his chair and glared at Chang. He slapped the papers on his desk and shouted, "In this letter your general in Taipan tells me of your military training and schooling in Europe. It says you're an officer, a captain yet. What kind of army does General Zeng Gudfan have? Your actions show you should not be a private, let alone an officer. What made you think you have the authority to declare war against the Indians?"

Chang rudely sat with mouth agape. Why was the tong so angry? What could Chang have done differently? He had shown the bloodthirsty Indians that the Chinese would fight if provoked. He did what a soldier is trained to do. Chang answered, "I should be praised, not cursed, for standing up to them."

"Do you know what you've done Captain Chang? It took me months to get our people established here and convince the white gold miners that we are no threat. I set up a laundry. I built a café to feed those too lazy to cook for themselves. I bought several gold claims. Over eight hundred of our people work here. You probably destroyed in weeks what took us months to establish. Perhaps the Americans will deport us now."

Chang stuttered, "W-what? Someone has to stand up to these savages or they will kill every one of our people. The only people they respect are fighters."

Zing Yong shouted angrily, "I don't belittle your bravery or fighting skills, but how could you be so stupid. What did you accomplish? You acted in revenge, nothing but pure revenge. White men say the Chinese all look alike. They can't tell one from another. Perhaps the Indians are the same. All our people will become targets because of your stupidity. The Indians will stop at nothing to get your scalp and all their warriors will shoot and scalp any Chinese person claim they killed you. All scalps look alike. What a mess you have gotten us into. Now, what can I do? How can I salvage our operation without getting all of our people killed?

"Captain Chang, go up to the sleeping room now and don't leave it until I tell you to! Your meals will be served to you there. If I need more information from you I'll go up there. Now get out of my sight!"

Chang stood and stumbled up the stairs as his mind churned. Instead of a returning hero, he had become a whore. Chang seethed, but the more he reflected, the more he realized the tong was right. By trying to win his peoples' scalps back from the Blackfoot, he had acted out of revenge. It was no act of compassion for the families of the dead Chinese as he had tried to make himself believe.

Several times during the next few days, Zing Yong questioned Chang about the Blackfoot Indians. The tong asked about the location of the Indian camp, the number of Indians, the name of the chief, the terrain and about the man Zeb. Eight days later, the tong summoned Chang to his office. Tong Zing Yong smiled, the first Chang had seen in eight days. "Captain, I owe you an apology. I am truly sorry for my rudeness, but I thought it best to keep you here for the protection of all our people.

"In the past few days," he continued, "I hired two old trappers who are familiar with the Blackfoot tribe. I sent them to the Indians' camp with a message for their chief. I proposed a meeting with the tribal elders to discuss what to do about you, our rogue Chinese warrior. Fortunately, your friend Zeb was still at their camp and he offered to be an intermediary. Two days ago, I met with their elders about twenty miles south of here. Zeb suggested I take a hundred of our best people armed with rifles. I also took a wagon loaded with barrels of our homemade gunpowder for a demonstration that Zeb thought might impress the Blackfoot. The chiefs saw our people armed with good rifles, and we blew up a barrel of gunpowder. Some of the Indians started to run, but their chiefs ordered them to stay. I told them that I have over eight hundred armed Chinese warriors, and I think they believed me. I also told them we have enough gunpowder to blow their village from the earth. The gunpowder demonstration helped convince them. After negotiations, we found a solution acceptable to both sides. They demand that the war you declared against them continue until they remove your scalp. It's a matter of honor. Chang's mouth went suddenly dry.

The tong continued, "If they stick to our agreement, and Zeb says they will, it might be a good thing for our people, but I may have sentenced you to death. You must stay here and continue your war. You alone will battle their entire tribe. Well, not the entire tribe, the chief seems to like you, but I am not sure any of the rest of the tribe does. The chief said he wishes more of his warriors were like you."

"Chief Three Fingers," said Chang.

"Yes. The chiefs promised that their warriors would harm no other Chinese people, no matter where they are. In return, we cannot fight beside you against the Blackfoot. They will allow our people to mine gold in their territory where the white man cannot go for some of the gunpowder we make. This might prove profitable to us, but you might be killed by Chinese gunpowder. Another condition is that you must wear a red headband at all times. They will shoot no Chinese people without the red headband. Anytime you are inside the tong house, they will not harm you. Chief Three Fingers said you are a man of honor and he knows you will always wear your headband outside of the tong house if you give your word that you will."

"Great," Chang groaned, "but what about the scalps? That is what this war was all about."

"The Blackfoot already returned the scalps of our people. Yours is the only one they want now. The Blackfoot also allowed us to recover the remains of our dead. They were cremated together with their scalps, and we returned the ashes to their families in China. The people I sent to collect the remains said that the Indians surrounded them, but did not interfere. Zeb says when the Blackfoot give their word they will die before breaking it. They believe fighting against the Yellow Chief is a great honor. They say the warrior who catches you and takes your scalp will become chief of their people. Zeb says he has never seen anything like it. The Indians quit hunting, fishing, and probably even making new Blackfoot babies to get themselves ready to hunt down the Yellow Chief. Even their women believe you are a spirit sent to test the strength of their warriors. Your friend Zeb thinks that if you stay and fight, you will be killed for sure. They will never let up. If it takes the last warrior in their tribe, they will hunt you until you are dead. Zeb thinks you will last longer if you study wilderness survival. You must learn to conceal your tracks and hide from the hunters or you won't live long."

"Zeb told me," Chang interjected, "that the Perce Nez Indians are better at tracking and concealment even than the Blackfoot. Perhaps we could hire a member of that tribe to teach me."

"Perhaps," smiled the tong. "At least maybe you can learn enough to stay alive for a few days. And I almost forgot, Zeb said he does not want to lose his weapons to the Blackfoot, so he will come by and retrieve them in a day or two."

Chang loved the rifle especially, and hated to give it up. He wondered what kinds of weapons would be available to him now. What kinds of weapons were sufficient to fight an entire tribe?

"I will not order you to continue this war. I can only say that if you do not stay and fight, many more of our Chinese people will die."

Chang smiled and said, "Honorable Tong, of course I'll fight them. I will do anything I can to make amends. I am a professional soldier and I took an oath to protect our people. I am grateful for a second chance. I was blinded by grief and I sought only revenge. I hope I never act without thinking again."

Chang heard a note of approval when Zing Yong said, "We will have a headband made and in the morning you will circulate in town. The Blackfoot scouts will surely see you and tell the tribe you are here. Plan this war carefully; I would hate to see you die." Changing the subject abruptly, the tong said, "Please come for dinner tonight with my wife and family. About sundown is best."

Chang said embarrassed, "I would be honored to meet your family but I don't know where you live."

Zing Yong chuckled, "I'm glad to hear it. I keep my work separated from my family. I do not want them bothered by folks who seek me. The large log house across the street from the livery stable is my home. Just walk in when you get there, we will be expecting you."

Just at sundown, Chang opened the door to the tong's house and stepped into a comfortably furnished room. A tantalizing aroma of freshly-baked bread made Chang's stomach growl. A long davenport and several overstuffed chairs grabbed his attention. Rawhide strips secured the leather upholstery, giving the chairs a pleasant rugged appearance. A round braided rug of brightly colored cloth covered most of the floor. Several oil lamps on small tables completed the decorations.

"Welcome to my home," Zing Yong greeted pleasantly as he entered the room. A servant took Chang's jacket. The tong said, "Please sit anywhere." He then called to someone in the next room. Shortly, an attractive Indian woman entered the room, accompanied by two young women and a boy. Chang stood. Zing Yong introduced he older woman, "This is my wife Starlight."

She shook Chang's hand and said, "It's so good to meet you Mister Chang. My husband speaks of you often." Starlight then introduced the younger women. "These are my children Cornsilk, Morning Bird and Running Fox."

Upon greeting Morning Bird, Chang felt beads of perspiration break out on his forehead. She was more than gorgeous. She was the most beautiful woman he had ever met. When he shook her hand, he forgot to release it. He gazed impolitely into her eyes, not hearing a word of introduction to the boy, who stood with outstretched hand. When Chang realized he was still shaking Morning Bird's hand he mumbled greetings. He was sure whatever he had just said was incomprehensible. He quickly released her hand and grasped the hand of Running Fox. Starlight announced, "Dinner is on the table. Shall we eat?" All filed into the dining room, Chang and Zing Yong were last.

Chang was so flustered he had no idea what foods were served. His mind was totally occupied with the beauty of Morning Bird. She might have been only eighteen or twenty, but definitely a grown woman. He was so smitten that anyone could have seen it. Her parents smiled indulgently as they finished their dessert. Starlight suggested they return to the sitting room and get comfortable while the youngsters cleared up the table. Chang regained his composure as he answered questions about his homeland and his travels in America. Conversation grew more comfortable as the evening progressed. Chang realized that Zing Yong's family had no knowledge of his recent experiences with the Blackfoot so he avoided the topic. He enjoyed the most pleasant evening he could ever remember having and when it grew late, he reluctantly excused himself and returned to his sleeping mat in the tong house.

The next morning, Chang had just finished dressing when Tong Zing Yong came in and said, "You are an early riser I see. That is good. Let us go down to breakfast then I have a few things I want you to do."

After going to the kitchen, they were the only two seated at a large table. After spooning up their meal, Zing Yong felt free to talk. "When you finish here I want you to go to my house. The women are sewing a red headband for you."

Chang's heart felt as if it had begun using his ribs for tom-toms at the prospect of getting to see Morning Bird again. He tossed and turned most of the night while thinking about her. "Last night," he said, "I could see that your family knew nothing about my experiences with the Indians."

"That is correct, and I want to keep it that way. After you get the headband, come back and we will take a stroll in town. We may even go to one of our gold mines upstream to show you off to the townsfolk. I hope a Blackfoot scout or two will see the Chinaman with a red band on his head. We need to make sure those Indians know you are still in the area. If you want to quit now I'll understand, I won't give a bad report to General Zeng."

"No sir, I will do my duty."

"You realize, I hope, that once you put on that headband you become a target for every Blackfoot warrior. Be assured, some of them are scouting Bannack as we speak."

It didn't take long for Chang to finish gulping down his breakfast on being ordered to Zing Yong's home. Hurrying to the dormitory he quickly changed into his best clothes. After washing his body and combing his neck-length hair, he was satisfied he looked his best. He rushed out the door and almost ran to the house of Zing Yong. Standing at the front door, he gave a tug on his trousers, tucked his shirt in tightly, flattened his hair with his hand and rapped on the door.

A window curtain parted and the door opened a moment later. Chang stood smiling, expecting to see Morning Bird. He quickly wiped a disappointed frown from his face when he saw Running Fox at the door. The boy greeted Chang by saying, "Come in Mister Chang." Chang followed Running Fox through the kitchen and into a small bedroom. The décor, from the dainty gingham curtains to the tasteful paintings to the frilly bed quilt, revealed the touch of tasteful feminine hand. Near the foot of the bed sat three women busily sewing and ironing. Upon seeing Chang enter, they stopped. Starlight exclaimed, "Mister Chang, we didn't expect you so early. Please sit," she said, pointing toward a wooden chair. "My husband told me what you want a red headband. Isn't that a strange request for a Chinese Captain? You will look like one of us Indians," she flashed a beautiful white smile that Chang immediately returned. "There are several shades of red." Gesturing toward Morning Bird she continued, "Morning Bird will show you the cloth. Tell her what you need and we will make it for you."

Chang was about to say that it need be nothing special, but luckily, he caught himself. This was his chance to talk with Morning Bird. He saw a wisp of a smile on the mother's face and he understood that this is what she intended all along. Chang stood and went to Morning Bird's side. Her scent was inebriating. Her shimmering black hair came just to his chin. In all ways she seemed perfect. He was living a dream. Her penetrating eyes, dark eyebrows and eyelashes, small upturned nose and narrow heart-shaped lips completed the dream, although as a professional soldier, he never expected the dream to come true.

Morning Bird's Indian ancestry was plainly evident in the reddish tinge it cast upon her pale yellow skin. She carried herself proudly and when she coyly flashed intelligent eyes at him, he knew he would do anything for her. Morning Bird brushed against his hand as she laid out several wide strips of red cloth on the table. The touch sent a thrill through his body he had never experienced before. "Why do you need red? We have plenty of other nice colors."

Chang pointed out a wide strip of bright red cloth and said, "This will do. Your father told me to wear a red headband."

"Why does he want you to do that?"

"Among other things, I suppose it shows our people I am not a laborer, so they will not ask me to help with their work projects. It might even help me do my job."

"What is your job?"

"Your father can tell you what it is if he wants to, but I am not allowed."

"How exciting, a secret mission."

"It is secret, but not that exciting."

It seemed to take only a minute for the three women to trim and sew up a simple cloth headband. Tying it tightly at the back of his head, Chang made sure it didn't interfere with his vision or hearing in any way. "Perfect," he said. "If it's not too much trouble could you make another in case I lose this one?" After the women made second headband, one of the hardest things he had ever had to do was to say goodbye. He told Starlight, "Zing Yong is waiting for me so I had better go. Thank you again for the headbands and for the wonderful dinner you served last night."

"You are very welcome young man," answered Starlight.

Morning Bird accompanied Chang to the door. He kept thinking, I do not wish to leave, I do not wish to leave, but he forced himself out the door. It wouldn't be fair to Morning Bird to pretend there was any future for them. After all, he probably wouldn't last out the week, let alone several years. Chang wore the headband to Zing Yong's office. Referring to the headband, the tong said, "It's bright enough for the Blackfoot to pick you off from 400 yards with a decent rifle. I don't feel good about doing this; it's like singling a sheep out to be slaughtered."

"Excuse me for saying so," said Chang, "but you seem a little more concerned about me today than you did yesterday."

"Well, my children seem to care for you. Besides, this war seems so foolish. You would think those Indians had more important things to do than chase down and kill a lone Chinese man. How can we stop this?"

"It may have gone too far to stop already."

The tong sighed, "It is time to go."

The two men went out the front door of the tong house and walked downhill toward the north bank of Grasshopper Creek. They could see the town of Bannack spread out below him. Huge piles of rocks lay on the banks of the creek. They had been removed to expose the bedrock where heavy ingots of gold would have settled. Hundreds of people of all races stooped over the bank of the creek washing gravel in their gold pans. Others shoveled sand and gravel into long wooden boxes. The water flowed through them, washing the lighter material away, and leaving the heavier gold particles in the bottoms. Some people struggled with large rocks, placing them beside the creek to get them out of the way. The scene reminded Chang of an anthill—people scurried everywhere, satiated by the lure of instant riches.

Main Street, nothing but a wide dusty road, sat several hundred yards above the creek bank. It followed the channel upstream until it disappeared behind a steep hill and continued to Virginia City some sixty miles to the east. Here at the base of the eastern hills the town of Bannack sprang up quickly because it was near the richest part of Grasshopper Creek, the current gold capital of the United States. Both sides of the road from the base of the eastern hills for about a mile downstream were crowded with structures made of any materials the owners could get their hands on. Ramshackle lean-tos, tents, dugouts and log cabins crowded together facing the road. Many shared a wall. Prospectors threw the town together with no prior planning. Each prospector simply wanted to search for gold as quickly as possible.

In contrast to the shacks were the half dozen permanent structures made of well-fitted local stone, brick and hand-sawn lumber. The six buildings all had ten-foot wide wooden porches beginning at the street and joined with high false front walls where the names of the businesses were hand painted. One of the buildings was a hardware store and miners' supply business and another was a large hotel. The rest were saloons.

The road was choked with traffic. Ore wagons, buggies, horses, cattle and hoards of people churned clouds of thick red dust. Dodging traffic, Chang and Zing Yong darted across the road and returned to the creek to watch the mining activity. Chang was amazed by Zing Yong's memory for names and faces. As they greeted individuals or groups of men, Chinese or white, the tong greeted each by name and inquired about their private affairs. Everyone seemed to know the tong.

Zing Yong led Chang upstream to the far end of town. Stopping in the shade of one of the last buildings in town, Zing Yong said, "Amazing, isn't it? A year ago, this was nothing but sagebrush. Now look at it. I think this gold rush is as big as the California discoveries were twenty years ago. There are over a hundred new people coming into the basin every day, and not all of them are honest gold miners. The saloons popping up in town bring in all kinds of riff-raff. Gamblers, thieves, bandits, prostitutess, we have them all. They have one thing in mind, to separate the gold from the miners. It is almost impossible to ship gold out of the territory. Bandits steal most of it within twenty miles of town. I hoped you might snoop around and find out whom these bandits are." Shading his eyes with his hand, he pointed toward a hill on the other side of the creek and said, "There are two horses there. The horses have no saddles."

Chang remarked, "Those are appaloosa warhorses. They must belong to Blackfoot scouts looking for me." Seeing movement, Chang threw himself against Zing Yong knocking him to the ground. Chang dragged the tong behind the miner's shanty as the thuds of two arrows sounded above him. Both arrows imbedded themselves in the side of the building. Jumping up to look, Chang saw two Indians running up the slope toward the horses. As Zing Yong got to his feet, he and Chang saw the two Indians sitting atop their horses. The four men stared at each other for a few seconds before the Indians turned their mounts and trotted up the slope and out of sight.

Chang said, "The red headband got their attention. Now they will inform their people you are here. You know," he continued, "those warriors are pretty good shots with bows and arrows at over fifty yards." Chang pulled the arrows out of the side of the building. Two miners jogged toward them and began shouting. Chang said, "They probably saw what happened. I'll let you explain this to them. If I say anything it will draw more attention to me."

Zing Yong smiled and replied, "You're learning Chang, you're learning."

As expected, the two miners approached. One inquired, "Was those redskins shooting arrows at you fellas? If they was, we need to catch and hang them savages."

"No," Zing Yong replied, "These are hunting arrows. They were shooting at a jackrabbit. I think they were hungry."

This explanation seemed to satisfy the minors' curiosity. As they turned to leave, one of them said, "If they do something like this again, you let us know and we'll put a stop to it real quick like."

As the two Chinese men returned to the tong house, Chang chuckled and said, "You handled that well. I don't think they will be sounding the alarm that the Indians are attacking the town. I think the big one just wanted an arrow." He tossed both arrows to Zing Yong. Entering the office, they were surprised to see Zeb leaning back in Zing Yong's chair. Zeb gave a friendly wave and said, "Howdy pard, I come to get my guns." Zeb stood, walked over to Chang and gave him a bear hug.

-SIX-

North America   October 1862

Montana Territory

Bannack

After greeting Chang and Zing Yong, Zeb sat in a chair near the tong's desk. Zing Yong settled himself in his chair, looked over at Zeb and said, "It is good to see you again. I did not expect you for another day or so.

"I got me a good horse—runs real good. Got me here quicker than fresh-sneezed hog snot."

"Is the agreement we made with those Indians still valid?" asked the tong.

Zeb leaned back in his chair and said, "I don't rightly know how to answer that question. Zing Yong, you sending them two fellers to their camp and getting that meeting with 'em was the smartest thing you ever could of done. You saved the scalps of a whole gaggle of Chinamen—Indians and white folks too for that matter. Since you people all look alike," Zeb smiled and winked, "I figured they was going to kill every yellow man they could find just hoping one of 'em was the Yellow Chief."

Zing Yong interrupted, "That's why I wanted to meet with them. I wanted to know if I could buy them off, trade them something. I was even prepared to turn Chang over to them to prevent another Chinese massacre."

Chang said, "Maybe I should still turn myself over to them to stop this nonsense right now."

"No, the time for that is past," Zing Yong replied, "I want you to stay alive if you can. Perhaps they will decide to call it quits when the weather gets colder."

Zeb said, "You might be right, if they get cold and hungry enough their squaws might tell 'em to stop, but probably not till they eat their last dog. It was smart thinking, you bringing all them Chinese folks armed with good guns to that powwow. When you blew up that barrel of gunpowder and told 'em you had a lot more they started to listen to what you was saying. Them Blackfoot elders and their warriors hashed out what all you folks talked about at your powwow. They asked me to come up here and tell you that they don't want to fight all the yellow men. I guess the tong done told you what the agreement was?" Zeb asked Chang, who nodded in the affirmative.

Sitting upright in his chair Zeb continued, "Now that I brung you this message, I'll tell you I was real glad to get out of their camp. They was driving me crazy. Ever since they came back from that powwow none of 'em can talk of nothing but slicing you up into itsy bitsy pieces. They all want to be chief. They've been beating on their war drums and dancing around their scalp poles day and night. Even their squaws has got caught up in it, dancing and chanting till they drop from exhaustion. They gone plumb loco."

Chang replied, "I can't think of an honorable way out, but I don't want to kill any more of them. Retrieving the scalps is no longer an issue so all I can think of is to make life miserable for them and try to stay out of their way until they get tired of hunting me. Both of you told me I need to learn how to move around in this country without being caught. Zeb you're real good at tracking, could you teach me enough to get by?"

Zeb replied, "No, it wouldn't work, I could show you a few things, but it'd take an Injun to show you how to do it right. I know a couple of trappers here in town who know every Injun around these parts. It was them two what come to the Blackfoot village to request your powwow. They might help you out. If I live to be a hundred, I will never understand how them red devils think. To them this is all a big happy game. If a white man killed half as many folks as Chang has, we would lynch him in the nearest tree and that would be the end of it. Not them. They make a big thing out of it and feast, dance and brag of how their going to catch up to you. But I ain't going nowheres yet. I'll stick around for a day or two, get my guns from Chang and mosey back up and tell 'em the war is still on."

Chang asked, "How many of their people did I kill Zeb? I hope it wasn't more than three. There were two at the cliff and one with the horse."

"Three?" Zeb questioned. "Must be something wrong with your tabulator. You killed them three, seven got blowed to bits by the guns you turned into bombs. Two others lived, but were in real bad shape afterward. That feller who fell on the spear point kicked the bucket and you shot one off a horse who was trampled to death. That's a dozen by my count. If you figured on revenge for the Chinamen they killed, you're ahead in the game."

Chang groaned.

Zing Yong said, "I think we covered about everything. My wife is making a good supper for us so if Chang will show you the dormitory you can stay at the tong house. I'll see you at my house at sundown. Oh, Captain Chang, when you get Zeb settled down would you come back down and see me, there is a matter I would like to discuss with you."

Chang stood and Zeb followed him to the dormitory. After showing Zeb the sleeping mats, and where to wash up, Chang offered, "Do you want me to fetch your pack from the front porch?"

Zeb said, "Nah, I ain't so old that I can't manage that."

Chang went to see Zing Yong. The tong looked up from some papers he was studying as Chang approached. The tong coughed, apparently searching for words. At last he said, "Captain Chang, I have a small problem that perhaps you could help me with. It's a problem I don't want to get out of hand."

Chang looked at him and said, "Of course, I'll be glad to help if I can."

Zing Yong said, "You met my family last night and I'm sure you noticed my older daughter, Morning Bird, she's a very impressionable young lady, barely out of her teens."

"Yes sir," Chang replied.

She seems to be quite taken by you, Captain." Chang felt his face light up. The tong continued, "I want you to discourage any of her advances toward you. I told her not to consider a military man for a companion. It is far too dangerous an occupation." Chang wasn't sure how to reply. "And please don't mention our conversation to her, the tong continued."

Chang was crestfallen. His mind churned. He hadn't made any ungentlemanly advances toward Morning Bird, but he knew she was interested in him, and his interest in her went far beyond friendship.

Zeb sat at one of the tables cleaning his rifle. Looking up as Chang came in he said, "You know pardner, you made a mess of my gun. If you don't keep her clean the Good Book says she's going to rise up and smite you, er, the Christian book, he hastily added."

Chang tried to look happier than he felt. He chuckled and said, " I did clean your weapons, and I'm quite familiar with the Christian Bible. It has no instructions about cleaning your rifle.

"You know about the Bible?"

I studied the doctrine of many religions. They are similar but different."

"How so?"

"Each professes the existence of a higher power only in different ways."

After supper, Zeb was amusing everyone with tales of his travels and adventures as a trapper and gold miner. Chang ached to talk to Morning Bird in private but instead stayed his distance from her. He stiffly answered questions from others, but paid little attention to the conversation. At the end of the evening, Zeb and Chang thanked the women for the fine meal, then returned to the tong house. In the dormitory, they pulled up chairs and sat. "I can't ever remember having a tastier feed," Zeb said. "No wonder Zing Yong is so chubby."

"Yes," Chang said without enthusiasm.

"I noticed that pretty young lady making eyes at you. If some young gal looked at me like that I think I would be thinking about a stroll in the moonlight about now." After looking at the frown on Chang's face, Zeb continued, "Now maybe that thought has already crossed your mind."

Suddenly Zing Yong came bounced in the room, pulled a chair up alongside Zeb and said, "Captain Chang, perhaps I came down too hard on you! After you left, Morning Bird came down on me with both feet. If I live to be a hundred, I'll never understand women. First thing she said was for me to, and these are her words, 'Mind your own business father.' She says she will see and talk to anyone she pleases and for me to stay out of her business. Now you tell me what brought that on. I didn't say anything to her about you and I didn't hear you say anything to her. So how did she know I told you to keep your distance?"

"So that's where it's at," Zeb chuckled. I sensed something was going on. You ever hear of women's intuition Zing Yong? You'd better pay attention to it. It's why a man can't never get away with a good lie to a woman. Ha!" he exclaimed. "If you want her to stay away from Chang here you sure don't get the job done by ordering her to. More than likely it'll just exactly the opposing effect." Zeb chuckled and pointed out to Zing Yong the normal pale yellow face of Chang was now a brick red. They both laughed.

Zing Yong said, "But that is not why I came here. We have to figure out what Chang is going to do. He can't hide up here forever."

Zeb leaned back in his chair and said, "I've been giving this problem some thought. As I see it, them varmints knows right where Chang is. If them sneaky critters get close enough to shoot an arrow at him right here in town, he's going to step out on the porch one of these mornings and end up with a tomahawk hairdo. I think he should head up to the Nez Perce camp and tell 'em what he wants and why. Since they ain't on good terms with the Blackfoot, maybe they'll give him the learning he needs. They might do it for no other reason than to irritate the Blackfoot.

"First we got to figure out how to get Chang up there without getting his hair parted a mite too deep. The way I figure it, he is on his honor not to take that red headband off his head whenever he is out, but that don't mean somebody like me can't wear one of them things too. If I was to dress like him with a headband on my head, I could get around town and maybe go out in the diggings. If I get myself seen prowling around, but not too closely by anyone, maybe I could fool 'em long enough for Chang here to sneak out of town and get ahead of 'em a day or two. Once they find out how you tricked 'em they won't think you acted dishonorably. They will think you done the smart thing. If either of you fellers got a better idea let's hear it."

Chang and Zing Yong considered this before Zing Yong said, "It might work but you can't be the decoy Zeb. You are our go-between so you can't take sides. I'm too rotund to impersonate Chang," the tong said laughing and patting his ample midsection, "but I know someone who will do it if Zeb accompanies him to keep him from being scalped."

Chang stated, "I wanted to leave town, but did not know how to get out undetected. I thought I would make a run for it. Yours is a better idea. I'll need weapons too. Maybe a good rifle and pistol like Zeb's."

"Yes, you've got to get a good rifle, but I doubt there's none like mine around here. Maybe you should get one of them new repeating guns. They don't have the range or accuracy of my Hawkins but you can get shots off quicker. It'd be better than anything the Injuns have. You'll need a couple of packhorses with trading supplies. It will slow you down some but might make it easier to parlay with 'em. I'll poke around town with our redheaded decoy a day or so but I think you better get started at sundown tomorrow.

"I'll make up a list of trade supplies and maybe Zing Yong can get them. Besides the packhorses, you'll need a good riding horse. I'll buy your weapons, nobody will question me buying 'em but they would damn sure remember you, especially with that red rag on your head. I'll need to get some money or gold to buy 'em though, I'm plumb near broke. Do you want a saddle like I got? Makes it a lot easier on your legs than riding bareback."

Chang said, "Don't buy a horse. I will use the little appaloosa I rode in on and put a blanket on its back like the Indians do. If I am going to learn to live like an Indian, I had better start acting like one. Besides, it is a lot less trouble if I don't have to saddle up a frisky horse in an emergency.

Zing Yong replied, "I'll get gold to buy what you need. Gold is the only kind of money the people in town will take anyway. It is getting late, so I am going home to see if Morning Bird has simmered down. I'll talke to you tomorrow."

－　　－　　－

After breakfast the next morning, Zeb said, "You stay here while I go see what kind of guns I can find. I've got enough gold on me to pay for them. Zing Yong can pay me back later."

After Zeb left, Chang went to the horse stable behind the house to check on the appaloosa. He picked out two strong packhorses and led them into the barn where he fed and watered them. Zing Yong was in his office when Chang returned. Chang informed him, "Zeb went to buy weapons. Here is the list of goods I need."

After looking the list over, Zing Yong said, "I will get these things. Stay inside until Zeb gets back."

An hour later Zeb returned with a long blanket roll. He laid it on Zing Yong's desk, where he unrolled it to reveal a short rifle and a pistol. He tossed the rifle to Chang and said, "That's one of the nicest guns I ever seen. The feller that sells 'em says you can load her up on Sunday and shoot all week. Them two trapper fellers swears by 'em. The rifle is short range but accurate to 200 yards. It's called a Henry and it loads up with these new metal cartridges." He tossed a round to Chang for examination. "Forty-five caliber, holds eleven rounds under the barrel. This here lever jacks a new cartridge into the barrel after you shoot one. It's fast. I shot up ten bullets in three or four seconds." Pointing at a pistol laying on the blanket he continued, "This here is a Colt pistol. It's a six-shot revolver that fires the same caliber bullets the rifle does. Makes it convenient. You don't have to be looking for different sized bullets to load your weapons."

It was well after noon before they finished packing everything in the two packsaddles and carried them out to the stable. Zeb looked the two packhorses over and nodded his approval then went back in the house and brought out the rifle scabbard. He said, "This gun scabbard is meant to hang from a saddle but you can hang it around your horse's neck. It will keep your rifle handy. The bag on the other side will hold a lot of gear. Looks like that's about it, unless can you think of anything else."

Chang replied, "I would like to buy that jacket I got from you. The pockets hold my pistol and ammo."

"Buy it" It's yours. I never did like it much anyway.

"Thank you," said Chang, meaning it.

"I think we should take a stroll around town and let you be seen again. I sure hope we can pull this off. A couple days head start can make a lot of difference. I need to draw you a map of where the Nez Perce camp is. I'll show you where the Crow and the Sioux are camped in case the Nez Perce don't want you around, or in case you can't get to the Nez Perce. I hope them Nez Perce will help you out 'cause almost all of 'em speak good English." The two men went back in the house where Chang tied on the headband. They then headed out the door and into town.

They stopped across the street from one of the saloons where Zeb stood licking his lips. "I'm kind of parched." A hitching post stood just in front of a long sloping roof covering the saloon's porch. On each side of the saloon entrance, a bench sat against the front wall of the edifice where several men sat watching the outdoor bustle. People, horses, and wagons congested the street. Just as Chang and Zeb attempted to cross the road, a wagon lumbered forward, forcing them to leap to the porch as the driver shouted obscenities. Zeb gasped exasperatedly as he glared at the wagon. After a moment he looked at Chang, smiled and said, "I suppose it won't do no harm go in and look the place over."

"I suppose not," agreed Chang.

Pushing through the double doors the two men went inside. A long bar stood at the far end of the large room, behind which a plate mirror was mounted to the wall. Shelves held more bottles of whiskey than Chang had ever seen in one place before. Even this early in the day the saloon business was booming. Gamblers sat at most of the tables. Most of the card players were obviously miners but at nearly every table sat a professional gambler, distinguished by a long dark jacket, starched white shirt and bow tie. People stood side by side, backs to the bar, most with glass in hand watching the doings at the gambling tables.

"Hows about a snort?" Zeb asked. He pushed his way toward the bar, followed by Chang. A drunk leaning against the bar grabbed Chang's arm and twisted him so they were face to face. The inebriated man blurted out, "What the hell is this Chink doing in here?" With a laugh, the drunk pulled a pistol from the waistband of his trousers and yelled, "Let's see if I can teach this dumb Chinaman to dance." Pointing the gun at Chang's feet, he pulled the trigger. The resulting explosion was deafening in the enclosed room. When a second shot rang out the room was in shambles as tables and chairs overturned from people diving for cover.

The bartender grabbed a shotgun and leapt over the bar, but before he could do anything else Chang kicked the drunk in the crotch. As the miner doubled over, Chang gave a vicious blow to the side of the head with the edge of his hand. As the miner dropped unconscious to the floor, Chang kicked his pistol away. The captain then pulled the drunk to his feet and dumped him in a chair. Seeing no other threats, Chang checked the drunk to make sure he wasn't hurt too badly. He told the bartender, "Bring him a drink on me," and tossed a gold nugget on the table.

The bartender gasped, "Wow, I ain't never seen a gent move as fast as you. Don't you worry none, I won't let him shoot at you again." He lifted the drunk off the chair, dragged him to the door and shoved him outside.

A few other miners mumbled and began fingering the grips of their handguns. Zeb eased over to Chang's side and said, "You done real good there pardner but I think we best get out of here before somebody else wants to see if you can dance."

Chang looked around at the disgruntled faces and commented, "I think you are right, I need my feet." The two men walked outside, stepping over the still unconscious miner en route to the street.

They dodged traffic while crossing. Zeb spoke first, "You sure enough got yourself some attention. The news'll spread, even to the Blackfoot."

As they walked, Chang heard a familiar voice calling, "So there you are, I've been looking for you." It was Zing Yong, and he quickly caught up with the others. "I think we should be seen talking to folks down in the goldfield, the Blackfoot are likely to have scouts there."

As they walked toward the ever-busy gold mines, Zeb told Zing Yong about the fracas at the saloon. He continued, "I don't think it will affect our plan none for getting Chang out of town."

Zing Yong shook his head and said, "You know, Chang you are just like a magnet, except you attract lead. It seems everyone wants to take a shot at you."

Chang shrugged, "It must be my charismatic personality."

"Most definitely," the tong laughed. "It even affects my family. I told my wife that you would be out of town on business for a few days and she insisted on making another supper for you two this evening. I'm going to go broke feeding you if you don't get out of town soon. The three men stopped to talk with several miners they passed then circled back to the road and returned to town.

As they passed the saloon where the drunk accosted Chang, the drunk was no longer lying on the porch. Zeb stopped and said, "I think I'll get that drink now. I'll see you back at the dormitory Chang. I don't dare take you in with me again, I might never get me a drink."

Zing Yong also excused himself. "I have work to do so I will see you this evening."

Chang stood in the shade of a shanty and watched Zing Yong walk away. He was preparing to continue his walk through town when suddenly a flash erupted from the doorway of a small lean-to across the street, immediately followed by a whoomp near his feet. Someone had shot at him, and he wasn't even armed. Chang sprinted across the street and flew through the shack's entrance door onto a surprised Indian frantically trying to reload his musket. Chang tore the gun from his hands and smashed it against the ground. He grabbed the Indian's long braided hair and was about to pummel him when he saw that the Indian was just a lad, probably in his teens. Chang assumed the boy was trying to make a name for himself in the tribe by coming here alone to kill the Yellow Chief. Chang tossed the shattered musket at the boy and turned in disgust to walk back to the tong house.

Chang shook in anger. How could the Blackfoot people encourage these acts by their young men? He stopped to watch the young Indian scamper into the hills. Chang was relieved he hadn't killed the young fool. Chang had a good view of most of the town and apparently, everyone was too busy to pay attention to a single gunshot. He shook his head in disgust as he turned and walked back to the tong house.

When Zeb returned to the tong house an hour later he was feeling no pain. He bellowed, "I could of got myself soused down there."

"Didn't you?" asked Chang.

"Naw, I used control. I didn't want to be in bad shape for dinner tonight. Everybody wanted to buy me a drink, even that feller that shot at you set one up for me--says he's real glad he didn't hurt you. The bartender told everyone you was like a rattlesnake—struck fast and hard then got the hell out of the way." Chang told Zeb, "So I am a hero to the men in the bar because I knocked out a drunk, but the other people in town do not care enough to see if I was injured by an Indian. Maybe I should return to China. At least people there want to kill each other for..." then remembering the wars among the people of China he said, "Maybe everyone is the same everywhere."

"What are you yammering about?"

"Nothing, lie down and sleep it off. We have to leave soon."

"Bu you were really something." Zeb's words slowed and slurred even more. "I think you was...," but Zeb passed out before he could finish the sentence.

—   —   —

Chang woke Zeb in time to head to dinner. As Zeb arose he groaned and reached for his head. "I must have had a few more drinks than I thought," he said.

A few minutes later Chang and Zeb were knocking at the tong's front door. Morning Bird ushered them in, took their jackets and invited them to sit. She told them, "Dinner is not ready yet. The bread dough did not rise." The announcement didn't bother Chang at all, especially when Morning Bird sat beside him.

No sooner had they been seated than Running Fox entered the room and said, "Father sent word he will be late. Someone's hurt at a mine."

Starlight suggested that Morning Bird show the men the garden while they waited. Morning Bird led them out the kitchen door to the backyard where a tidy garden lay. Morning Bird described the rows of vegetables. Zeb gave a little moan, and rubbed his head. He excused himself saying, I ain't much into dirt farming. He returned inside leaving Morning Bird and Chang alone. Knowing their time was limited, Chang wanted to blurt out his feelings for Morning Bird, and yet he couldn't rush things. Instead, he took a pea pod, opened it and said, "See how comfortably the peas live under the same roof?"

Morning Bird answered, "I would be at peace sharing a roof with you." Chang smiled so broadly he felt his face would crack. They looked deeply into each other's eyes, sharing their love openly then they embraced. When Morning Bird shuddered, Chang looked into her face. A single tear migrated gently along the curve of her cheek. Neither said anything for a few minutes. They simply gloried in each other's presence. When at last they spoke, they discussed their hopes for the future.

It seemed but a moment later when Zing Yong found them standing close together in a dark area of the garden and announced, "Dinner is ready. If you two have seen all there is to see of the garden in the dark, let's eat." Morning Bird and Chang smiled. Hand in hand, they followed the tong inside.

After dinner, the group retired to the parlor. After a long, pleasant discussion, the hour came for Zeb and Chang to take their leave. That is when Zing Yong chose to announce that Chang would be leaving town for a few days. Looking at his wife said, "At least you will have one less mouth to feed."

Starlight replied pleasantly, "It's been a real pleasure to cook for our friends. I hope Captain Chang isn't gone too long."

"Where are you going?" Morning Bird interrupted, flushed with anger.

Chang answered, "I want to find the Nez Perce Indians to request permission for our Chinese people to gold on their land." Looking deeply into Morning Bird's eyes he said, "I do not know how long it will take me. Not too long, I hope." To Starlight he said, "I will miss your marvelous cooking."

Zeb stood and rubbed his head again. He said, "Well, it's getting too late for this old coot to be up and about so I think I'll just thank you again for supper and mosey on back to the tong house."

Reluctantly, Chang said that he had better be leaving too. He said goodnight to the family as Morning Bird handed him his jacket. He was surprised when Zing Yong suggested that Morning Bird show him to the front gate. Once outside, Morning Bird demanded, "Why did you not tell me you are leaving? I feel like such a fool."

"I hope I will be gone only a few weeks," said Chang.

"Weeks?" Morning Bird nearly shouted.

"I will return as soon as I can, I promise." He took Morning Bird in his arms and held her longingly. He whispered goodbye, and Morning Bird sobbed and ran into the house. Chang felt his eyes burn with tears, something he had not felt since he was a child. After a last longing glance at the house, he turned and started toward the tong house.

When Chang entered to the dormitory, Zeb and Zing Yong were there. "Tong Zing Yong, sir, I did not know you were here," said Chang.

"I did not care to disturb you two young ones. Besides, I only arrived just before you."

Realization dawned on Chang. "You were watching us?"

"Captain Chang, Morning Bird is my eldest child. What would you expect of a caring father?"

Zeb was busy tying one of Chang's two traveling packs. He said, "Chang, you're as flustered as the chicken that got away from the fox." Chang's face felt flushed. Zing Yong smiled slyly.

Zeb handed Chang a small paper, telling him, "This is a list of everything in each pack so you don't have to go through 'em both to find what you are looking for." He handed Chang his telescope and continued, "This comes in right handy at times. I'll get it back when you're all through with this Blackfoot business. I'll help you get your horses ready. You best get started. Every hour you can stay ahead of 'em might save you a lot of grief."

-SEVEN-

CHANG LED HIS horse from the barn and into the fenced corral outside. He tossed a small woolen blanket on the horse's back, and hung the rifle scabbard on the right side of the horse's neck just in front of the blanket. He hung a large pouch on the other side. It held drinking water, a bag of jerky and cartridges. He put his pistol and Zeb's telescope in the jacket pockets. Satisfied he had everything, he took the reins of his two packhorses from Zeb. The tong opened the corral gate. Chang gave them a nod as rode into the night. With the map Zeb had drawn for him firmly etched in his mind, Chang rode west on a well-used wagon road, figuring that would cover his tracks better than anything else. He stopped only to water his horses each time he crossed a stream.

About midday, he arrived at the junction of the north-south road, which was nothing more than a wide trail. He turned north. From here on, he would have to ride hard if he hoped to stay ahead of the Blackfoot warriors. They would be after him the moment they realized he had slipped away. At dusk, his horses were tired from the grueling trek, even after taking several stops to loosen their packsaddles and let them graze.

Coming to the summit of Lost Trail Pass, he veered into a dense stand of aspen trees. He dropped the packsaddles and tied the horses to

trees with long ropes. He searched with the telescope but saw no sign of Indians. At first light, he was already on the trail. The path soon bottomed out as it followed the eastern foothills. Late in the afternoon he encountered a long pack train coming south with supplies for the gold fields. Chang dismounted as he approached the first of the mules making up the pack train. A rider pulled off the trail and signaled to another rider to keep going. The first rider dismounted and said, "Howdy, stranger. My guess is either you're either a gold miner with a full poke heading out of the country or you gave up on the gold and are getting out anyway. I sure never expected to see a lone Chinaman out here on the trail."

Chang sensed no danger from this man. He chuckled, "Nope, no gold. I'm heading to Lewiston. You are the first traders I've seen on the trail since I left Bannack."

The trader slapped some of the dust off his clothes with his hat, looked over at the long string of pack animals going by and said, "I'm glad to hear that, I just might make a profit out of this venture yet."

When the last of the mules ambled by, the trader remounted. Before riding off he said, "I ran into a bunch of Sioux at Lolo Pass yesterday. I think they stole horses from the Nez Perce, so you best watch yourself. I had to give 'em one of my mules to eat so's they'd leave us alone. They dearly loves mule meat, but they're on the prod. If those Nez Perce catch up to 'em don't get yourself in the middle of it. They're headed off toward the Yellowstone to trade 'em to the Crow so I think you might bump into 'em."

It was well after dark when he came to the eastern end of the Lolo Trail, an ancient Indian trail that snaked over the rugged Bitterroot Mountains. Travelers coming from the east through the South Pass of the Rocky Mountains by wagon had to go south to Fort Hall and along the Snake River through the Blue Mountains and to the coast. On horseback, a rider could choose the Lolo Pass Trail. It was a much shorter route to the coast but no wagon could make it. Before starting up the pass, Chang pulled off the trail and rode up a small stream for a few hundred yards. There he dropped the packs off the horses, watered the horses well and tied them in a stand of trees. There was plenty of good grass for grazing. Chang wrapped himself in his blanket and dozed off.

Daylight found him climbing steeply. The few hours rest prepared him and his horses for a long tiring day. Several hours later, he descended the opposite side of the steep rocky slope. It was then he noticed one of his packhorses limping. He dismounted and led the horses on foot to the bottom of the hill. As soon as he could, he left the narrow trail and concealed the horses behind a dense stand of pine trees. He tied the horses loosely and dropped the packs from them. He examined the right rear leg of the limping horse and was relieved to a small sharp rock lodged in its hoof. He pried it out and noted no permanent damage. He thought how fortunate he was. If he lost a horse for any reason, he would have to leave the horse and pack where they stood.

He decided to let his horses graze and rest there after the arduous journey over the pass. He was sitting under a tree in the shade, when suddenly all three horses snorted nervously. Each horse looked up the trail it had trod. A moment later, Chang heard a commotion growing louder by the second. A string of horses spilled over the crest of the hill herded by a group of about ten Indian horsemen. They rode recklessly, yelling and urging the horses to greater speed with long willow switches. Chang retreated further into the trees with his horses and grabbed his rifle. He watched the horses descend the steep trail and gallop up the slope Chang had just came down. Kneeling for additional concealment, Chang watched the horses and Indians climb the steep trail and disappear over the crest. No sooner had he breathed a sigh of relief than a second group of riders appeared from the same direction as the first.

Staying well out of sight, Chang watched this second group of horsemen until they also disappeared from view. He thought it best to stay put for now. A few seconds later he heard gunshots echo through the hills. Chang didn't know one tribe from the next, but he assumed that the first Indians who passed must be the Sioux, who the trader had warned him about. He also assumed that those in hot pursuit were Nez Perce.

He was thankful he had stopped to check his horse as he sure didn't want to get mixed up in this fight. He listened to the sounds of the fierce battle on the other side of the hill. After all gunfire ceased he decided to see what was happening. He climbed up the slope, but most evidence of horses and riders was gone, except their dust. At the bottom of the slope, he saw a horse lying on the trail so he went for a better look. The horse was dead, but Chang found an Indian lying nearby. Chang rolled the man over and noticed he was still breathing. He had a nasty gash in his head and a bullet wound in his right shoulder. His right foot was bent over, obviously broken at the ankle.

The Indian was a slightly built elderly man, dressed in a long sleeved leather shirt, fringed along the sleeves. Below it, a leather skirt hung over fringed leggings. He also wore knee high moccasins. Chang jogged back to retrieve his appaloosa. When he returned he hefted the Indian face down over the horse's back, mounted up behind and rode back to where he had staked his horses. He pulled the Indian off the horse and laid the man on his back.

Chang thought it best to reset the man's foot while he was unconscious. Pulling his foot down and twisting it forward, he heard it grind into place. He cut two short stout sticks and bound them to the ankle to immobilize the foot. The bullet wound in the shoulder did not appear to be serious. No bones there were broken. He rinsed the shoulder and bound the wound with cloth from his pack. Finally, he cleaned the laceration in the Indian's forehead. The fall, rather than a bullet, apparently caused it.

Chang laid the Indian on some pine boughs then looked over his handy work. He wondered what to do next. He couldn't take the time to transport him if he wanted to stay ahead of the Blackfoot, but he couldn't leave him here or he would die. Then the Indian opened his eyes and saw Chang kneeling beside him. He tried to push himself up but fell back too weak to rise.

Chang poured a few drips of water in the old man's mouth. He coughed for a moment, then smiled. He looked at his foot then felt the bandages on his shoulder and head. Chang asked, "Do you speak English?"

The Indian started to speak but was interrupted by a now familiar sound to Chang—the whoosh and thunks of three arrows embedding themselves into a tree beside them. Chang grabbed his rifle and threw himself on the ground as he frantically searched for those who shot the arrows. He rolled away from the Indian but stopped when another arrow struck a tree just above his head. The injured Indian yelled something and another Indian, dressed similarly to the one Chang helped, stepped from behind a tree less than fifty feet away. The injured Indian pointed at Chang and said in perfect English, "Put your gun down and stand up, he won't shoot you." The old man struggled to sit up and leaned against a tree. He called the warrior over.

The warrior picked up Chang's rifle and motioned him to sit. Turning to the wounded Indian the newcomer said, "We thought you were dead, shot in the head like your horse."

"Where are the others?" the injured man asked.

"They are here. We came back to get your body before a bear did. Who is the yellow man?" he asked pointing at Chang.

"All I know is that he bound my injuries. That is not something he would do if he intended me harm." The wounded man made the loud chirping sound of an excited squirrel. Four more Indians materialized from the woods, bows or guns at the ready as they approached and surrounded Chang. "Who are you?" the wounded man asked. I've never spoken to a yellow man but I heard you speak English. Why are you helping me?"

"Where I come from," Chang said, "we tend the wounded whether they are enemies or not, but I do not believe you are my enemy. I was resting in this grove of trees when I saw you chasing the others along the trail. I heard gunshots and went to investigate. I found you and your dead horse on the trail and I brought you here to tend your wounds. My name is Chang. Now I would like to know who you are and why you chased those others with the horses."

"I'm Looking Glass," the wounded man replied, "Chief of the Nez Perce and these are some of my warriors. The Sioux stole some of our horses and we were trying to get them back." Chief Looking Glass told his warriors, "Start a fire so we can cook something to eat."

One of the warriors soon had a small fire started. Another Indian lifted a large leather bag from a horse and carried it to the fire. He emptied its contents on the ground and poked through the pile before removing several large chunks of filthy half-rotten meat. He speared them with green sticks and pushed them in the fire. He then put several dried fish on a nearby rock and sat back to cook the meat. Chief Looking Glass grimaced in pain, leaned back and told Chang to eat. The warriors pulled half-cooked or charred, meat from the fire, broke off chunks of iron-hard dried fish and gobbled them down.

Chang took a few bites, gagged them down and watched the others obviously enjoying their meal as the last scrap of food disappeared into the mouth of one of the warriors. Licking their fingers and belching loudly they all lay, resting contentedly. A minute or two later, one of them asked the chief, "We won't catch those Sioux tonight, so what do you want us to do?"

The chief leaned back against a tree and answered, "We will stay here until morning then return to our village." Looking at Chang, he asked, "Are you a trader with the gold diggers?"

It was dark when Chang finished telling his experiences with the Blackfoot and why he was so desperately seeking the Nez Perce Tribe. "I have heard," he said, "that the Nez Perce are the most skilled in the art of camouflage and have the best trackers anywhere. Would someone in your tribe teach me what I need to know?" All the warriors paid close attention as Chang spoke.

Chief Looking Glass laughed and said, "This Yellow Man has taken on a big job if he really means to fight our enemy the Blackfoot by himself." All the warriors laughed. Then the chief continued, "You don't need to worry about the Blackfoot attacking you here in our land. They are brave but not that brave. They are not fools."

Chang wanted to ask if the Sioux were fools for being on Perce Nez land and stealing their horses. However, he didn't want to offend the Perce Nez as he had the Blackfoot, so he said nothing.

Chief Looking Glass continued, "I believe you saved my life, so I will do what I can to save yours. If you will come to our village I will find someone to teach you how to fool the Blackfoot."

"Thank you," Chang said. "Thank you very much."

"I must ask you something," said the chief.

"Anything," said Chang.

"When you brought me here, did you tie these sticks on my foot so I could not run away from you?"

Chang was surprised at the question. He thought the Indians knew much about healing, but maybe those were other tribes. Chang answered, "When I found you laying on the trail your foot was broken and pointing backwards. To fix broken bones you must turn them back where they should be. I tied sticks to your ankle so the bones will not move while they heal. You should leave them there were many days. You will have to find a good stick to put under your arm and support your weight until your foot grows back together."

The chief looked at his foot and said, "I have seen people hurt like this before. The leg, foot, or arm turns black and then they die. I expect to die also. You are not a medicine man. You did not sing to the spirits or blow smoke on my foot to blind the spirits. You say I will walk again. If this is true you must be a great medicine man sent by the spirits to keep me alive."

Chang selected a tree branch with a well-formed fork. He cut and trimmed it with his knife, and had the chief stand and support himself against a tree while Chang cut the bottom at a comfortable length. Chang showed the chief how to brace the fork under his arm and walk around without putting weight on the broken foot. Chang was impressed with the chief's stamina. In spite of the pain, he mastered the use of the crutch.

Early the next morning a warrior rode into camp and reported to Chief Looking Glass that a large band of Blackfoot had ridden up to the base of the pass, met up with the horse-stealing Sioux and set up camp together. The messenger's companions would keep the chief updated.

The chief told Chang, "If the Blackfoot have war paint on them they will not be allowed to come up the pass into our Nez Perce country, so you are safe from them here. I have been thinking of your war with the Blackfoot. The Nez Perce are not at war with them so my people can't help you kill them. Last night you told me that the Blackfoot know you as Yellow Chief. It is a great honor to be a chief. They think highly of you. Before I tell my people to help you I must know what you will do if we refuse to help you. Have you considered that the Blackfoot will give us many horses if we give you to them?"

Chang replied, "I have considered where I might find help in learning the Indian ways. The Sioux, the Crow, and Cayuse might teach me but the Nez Perce are held in the highest regard. It is said that no one can hide from a Nez Perce and that no one can find a Nez Perce if he does not want to be found. I must learn how to do this if I want to fight this war in their own country and do more that run from them.

"I have been very lucky in this war so far but luck does not win a war and it will not keep me alive very long. I came here to seek the aid of the Nez Perce but if they won't help me I will ask the Crow or the Sioux for help."

"You are still very lucky, Yellow Chief. The Crow or the Sioux would give you to the Blackfoot for a horse or a wife in an instant. Do you understand what you are asking to learn? Our people speak with our hands and learn to follow tracks from the time they learn to walk. How long do you want to live with us to learn these things, six moons or twelve?"

Chang looked at him intently and replied, "One moon."

"That is not nearly long enough to learn our ways Yellow Chief."

— — —

Since Chief Looking Glass' horse was dead, he rode double with a warrior. He had trouble at first because he had always mounted a horse from his right foot but after several attempts, he managed to hoist himself up from the left side. As they followed the narrow trail through the mountains, Chang brought up the rear with his two packhorses.

It was getting dark when they passed from the foothills into a vast expanse of small rolling hills. The steeper slopes were covered with tall green fir and pine trees, and the bottomland was carpeted by lush grassy meadows. Coming to the edge of a large lake, they turned north along its shores until it got too dark to travel farther. They ate quickly, although Chang ate his own jerky this meal rather than the meat offered by the Perce Nez. He did, however, accepted a freshly caught fish from the lake.

Late next afternoon they rode into the village of Chief Looking Glass. They stopped near a long curiously made structure. It had thick walls of interwoven tree limbs and the roof was thatched with the same material. Small nearly square doorways were cut into the front wall every ten feet or so. Surrounding the building were about forty conical teepees similar to those of the Blackfoot.

The first thing Chang noticed different from the Blackfoot camp was the lack of noise and dust. He could hear people talking and moving about but there weren't any dogs. The only horses he could see were the ones they had ridden in on. A young boy darted out of one of the doorways to gather the droppings of one of the horses then ran back inside. The village grounds were clean and the entire camp was neatly laid out. With the aid of his walking stick, the chief hobbled to the last doorway. A crowd of warriors, women and children had gathered around as they dismounted, but even the greetings and questions were subdued. There was none of the hubbub of the Blackfoot village. Two men dropped Chang's two packs from his horses and set them near the chief. All the horses were then led from camp.

The chief waved Chang over to stand beside him as he spoke to the crowd. The chief called out, "My people, we came back without the horses the Sioux stole from us. I am sorry for that, but we will steal them back another time. I brought with me a yellow man who will live with us for a short time. He saved my life, so I want you to make him welcome to our village. Get your families and bring them and I will tell everyone at once why the yellow man is here."

As the people went to their lodges to round up their families, the chief told Chang, "Come with me." The two ducked to enter a door of the long lodge. As Chang's eyes adjusted to the dim light, he was surprised to see the lodge wasn't divided into single rooms as he had expected, but was one long room. Opposite each doorway was a fire pit and against the far wall were sleeping mats, clothing, pots, weapons, warm buffalo robes and other belongings. Several fires glowed in the pits. People sat on the ground or lay back on their robes.

Chang asked, "Are these all members of your family?"

"Yes, we all live here as you see us. Some of our people like my family and me prefer to live as our ancestors did, as one large family. Things have changed. Most of our tribe now lives in separate lodges. I will give you a lodge to stay in, but if my foot turns black and I die my people will send you away." Chief Looking Glass motioned Chang outside then hobbled out to sit on a stump that one of his young boys set up for him. Shortly a crowd of warriors assembled and set themselves in several rows in front of the chief. It must be their pecking order, Chang thought.

The chief stood, balanced himself on his crutch, and told his people, "This man is called Yellow Chief by the Blackfoot. He alone fights a war with them and wants to learn some of the tracking skills of the Nez Perce."

The tribe members laughed at the idea of this small yellow man fighting the entire Blackfoot tribe. They thought their chief was telling them a joke. The chief raised his hands. "What I say is true," he said. As the people realized the chief was serious, they grew silent.

One warrior asked, "Why are you at war with the Blackfoot?" When Chang told of the Blackfoot warriors he had killed and how he had done it, the Nez Perce grew enthusiastic. Almost all of them volunteered to show Chang what they could about tracking and camouflage.

Another warrior asked, "Where do you plan to fight them?" Chang answered all their questions one at a time. The discussion went on for over an hour. Finally the chief put an end to the questions by stating, "Our warrior Broken Bow will begin teaching Yellow Chief tomorrow evening, but we want him to know now that if he can't or won't do exactly as he is told, he will leave our village. We won't waste our time if he will not learn. It will not be fun. It will take much hard work. He must work from sunup to sundown to learn what he should know to survive in Blackfoot country. The meeting broke up and people headed off in all directions.

After the crowd dispersed, Chang set his two packs in front of the chief and said, "I brought these goods with me to pay the people who agreed to help me. They are yours now. If these things are not enough to pay for your efforts, I have gold to give you also. You know you can trade gold to the white men for anything. They have an incredible lust for gold."

The chief opened the packs and laid out their contents in front of him and said, "You have many fine things here. Our women will be pleased with the colored cloth and the beads. You must have put much thought in selecting these goods. My warriors think this war, one Yellow Man fighting the entire Blackfoot tribe, is futile. All the tribes in the country will laugh at the Blackfoot, but you can't win. It doesn't matter what we show you, it will not be enough. Eventually one of them will catch you and take your scalp, but my warriors want to see how long you will last so they will teach you well."

Chang walked through the camp meeting many of the Nez Perce warriors and their families. He was amazed at their friendliness and willingness to talk. All were interested in where he was from. Most already knew how Chang had tended the wounds of their chief.

Chang learned that Chief Looking Glass was the chief of this small village, one of three villages of the Nez Perce tribe. The largest and main village was that of Chief Joseph, further west over the mountains. The third village was the camp of Chief Lawyer, a day's ride to the north. The Nez Perce people were free to move from village to village if they chose to. Each band worked with or helped the others if they needed it. Almost all of them spoke good English and they seemed to get along well with the white men, having first met them when Lewis and Clark passed through their country some fifty years earlier.

The village came alive at daybreak. Smoke from cooking fires drifted from the tops of the teepee's and so much smoke seeped from the long lodge's roof, Chang thought is was on fire. He ran toward the lodge yelling for everyone to get out. Several people stopped too see what he was shouting about. Chang ran inside the lodge and realized that it was not on fire. There were no smoke vent holes through the roof, but even with six fires burning in the lodge, it wasn't smoky inside. The walls and ceiling of dry wood looked like a firetrap to Chang, but someone told him the lodge was made of fireproof wood, and the lodge was over eighty years old. All present had a good laugh at Chang's expense. He even laughed at himself.

Chang ate with the chief, and he was glad he did. The chief's wives cooked up small flat cakes of ground corn and fried strips of venison, both clean and fresh. Chang learned as much as he could of the people and their lives. He wanted to know how their minds worked—how they thought. He watched as the women pawed through his trade goods, marveling at bolts of cloth, needles, thread, beads and small mirrors. He noted that the chief set a few of the items aside. "Some of our women are too old or sick to come," he said. "I will save some for them."

As the women looked through the gifts in his packs, he saw several men leading a horse. It dragged a bundle of long slender poles. The men lashed the tops of the poles together and stood them upright to form the walls of a teepee. They covered the lodge with buffalo hides, after which the chief said, "This is your home for as long as you're with us, Yellow Chief. Our women will help you make a fire ring and bring you some sleeping robes. I think you should arrange it as you want to right now because starting in the morning you will be very busy doing other things."

In the early evening, several people sat in front of Chang's new lodge. Soon, nearly the entire village had assembled. Chang stood at the entrance wondering what was going on. Looking Glass hobbled over and sat near Chang. The chief said, "I've assembled the warriors who agreed to teach you the things you must learn, the others are here to watch." He pointed at a warrior and said, "This is Rolling Thunder." A man stood, walked over to look at Chang then sat beside the chief. "Rolling Thunder is one of our best scouts. There is nothing his eyes miss when he seeks enemies on the warpath. He agreed to be your teacher. Listen closely to all he tells you."

The warrior walked over to Chang, stared into his eyes, circled and examined him as if he were a horse. Rolling Thunder squeezed every muscle on Chang's body and said, "This Yellow Man is stronger than I thought he would be." To Chang he said, "I will teach you as fast as you can learn but the first time you don't do exactly what I tell you I will walk off. The second time I will not come back. I want you to ask questions when you don't understand—questions yes, arguments no. If you don't like my way of teaching you can walk away, but starting in the morning I am the only person that you will talk to with your tongue except for someone I choose to help you talk with your hands. Until I tell you differently, you will talk only with your hands, including to the chief, all children and the women who cook for you." Rolling Thunder then told the chief, "We will see just how strong this yellow man is, I doubt he will do well." The last statement displeased Chang, he was proud of his will power. When he made up his mind to do something, he did it.

After daylight, an elderly woman entered his lodge carrying a small pot of stew and handed it to him. "Thank you," said Chang. "What is your name?"

Before the woman answered, Rolling Thunder stormed in and shouted, "Shut your mouth! I don't want to hear a sound from you except when talking with me." He looked at the woman and spread his hands out making several odd shapes with his fingers. She raised her hands and moved her fingers in reply. "She says she hopes you enjoy your food," Rolling Thunder said as the woman left the lodge.

Chang was taken aback at this brusque greeting, but he ate every bit of stew. He would need all the strength he could get before the day was over. When he was finished eating, Rolling Thunder said, "I don't have time to train you in all I know. What I do without even thinking might be very hard for you to do at all, and I'm only going to show you a little of what all of our warriors know how to do with ease."

They walked out of the teepee and away from camp, stopping occasionally to examine a tree. He held his hands out and bent the two middle fingers in. He held the sign until Chang repeated it. Rolling Thunder continued pointing out objects and teaching Chang the signs for them. Stopping in a small meadow, the warrior asked Chang what he could see around them. Chang pointed out the obvious, trees, bushes, and rocks around them. Rolling Thunder pointed out squirrels, bees and anthills that Chang had missed. Rolling Thunder then told Chang, "Walk back to your lodge, then return here and see if you can find me. I will be within fifty feet of where we now stand."

Chang did as instructed, and when he returned to the spot where he left Rolling Thunder he looked in trees, behind bushes and everywhere else he could think of within a one hundred foot radius. After several minutes, he decided that the warrior was fooling him and had probably gone back to camp. Chang became irritated and began to walk back to camp when the ground erupted only five feet in front of him. Out leaped Rolling Thunder with a knife in his hand. Astonished, Chang was sure he walked over that spot several times. Rolling Thunder said, "Hiding is not hard to do if you know who you're hiding from."

Chang spent most of the day learning more hand signs, and examining tracks left by animals and moccasins. In the afternoon, Rolling Thunder pointed out a bush and a tree and said, "Stand between them and do not move until I tell you to."

When Chang was in position, the Indian moved behind him. Chang assumed he was being tested so he stood there trying to remain as motionless as possible. His muscles burned and he began to feel lightheaded from the lack of blood circulation, but he wanted Rolling Thunder to think he was doing well. It was well after dusk before the Indian spoke to Chang again. From a foot away Rolling Thunder said, "You did well, but I saw some movement. You've got to do better tomorrow. Return to your lodge and we will begin anew in the morning."

First thing the following morning, Chang was instructed to lie on his stomach out in the open. After hours of lying motionless, Chang pulled a large ant from his ear. His instructor immediately yelled at him, "The sting of an arrow will hurt much more than an ant. When I say don't move, I mean it!"

Chang limped back to his lodge. He ached all over. A young warrior met him there. The warrior observed, "You look like you met a pack of wolves."

Chang was about to answer, but remembered that he was not supposed to speak to anyone. He closed his mouth and glanced about to see where Rolling Thunder was hiding. Chang thought this must be a test to see if the Indian could catch him speaking to someone. The young warrior said, "Do not fear. Rolling Thunder said he would choose one other warrior with whom you may speak. I am that warrior." He sat with Chang for several hours teaching more hand signs.

The days passed slowly. By day, Chang learned from Rolling Thunder and by night, the young warrior taught the language of the hands. One evening the young warrior told, "You are much too slow. You must speak as the Indians do," but Chang could not do it quickly. Try as he might, he couldn't seem to get the hang of it. His hands moved slower than his tongue.

Over the next few weeks, Chang learned to remain motionless for hours at a time, to move at a crouch, and to worm his way on his stomach for several hundred feet. At times he changed positions so slowly that he was unaware of time. On other occasions, darting from position to another was best way to move. The training never let up except for sleep and short breaks for meals. One day melded into the next. Occasionally one of his instructors would take a break and assign someone else to teach for a day, but there were no breaks for Chang. Never once was he given a word of praise, but his stupidity was cursed regularly.

One morning as he followed antelope tracks he realized he had performed the same acts for weeks. He could follow animal tracks, but he still couldn't camouflage his own tracks even from even the Nez Perce children. He was disheartened. He worried that if he didn't make a move against the Blackfoot soon they might become frustrated and attack his people in the gold fields. He decided if he didn't learn more soon he would quit. He would have to get by on what he knew already. Rolling Thunder left for several days, leaving Chang in the charge of others. When Rolling Thunder returned, Chang told of his anxiety.

"Stay a few more days," the warrior said. "You're just beginning to get the feel of hiding your tracks and sign. We will talk more on this tomorrow." He then pointed toward a large rock on a hill and said, "Hike up there and I will see if I can find your tracks."

As Chang studied the route he would take to get there, the realization dawned that the two men had spoken by hand signs only. He could talk by hand nearly as well as he could by voice. Sitting on the rock, Chang watched Rolling Thunder follow his tracks. He stopped here and there to put a stick in the ground. Signaling Chang to join him, the Indian pointed out his mistakes. Here and there a tuft of grass was bent, or seeds from a bush had fallen to the ground where he had brushed against it. Chang could see his mistakes and shrugged in resignation, "I've tried hard to learn your ways, yet as I see it, I'm not getting any better at concealing my tracks now than I was the day I came to you for help."

The warrior looked at Chang and said, "You've learned much, Yellow Chief. You will never will be able to hide from the Nez Perce but I don't think there is a Blackfoot warrior anywhere who could follow your tracks." Chang was astonished. This was the first time Rolling Thunder had ever called him Yellow Chief, and it was the first praise he had heard. The warrior continued, "When you are in the Blackfoot country you must plan every move. Think as they do. See what they see. Your greatest weapon is your head. Know your objectives. It will be interesting to watch what you do."

For the rest of the day the captain practiced concealment in a shallow hole. He learned to dig the hole near the base of a bush, scatter the dirt, and put brush and rocks over himself to and make it look natural. He learned several little tricks, like laying rocks weathered side up and making broken twigs appear as if a bird had broken them. He learned as much as he could to leave no clues for sharp-eyed trackers. Returning to the village earlier than usual that day, Chang was surprised that his evening teacher did not come. The woman who brought him his meals spoke to him and said, "I am told that we can talk with our tongue instead of our hands. Does this mean you will be leaving us soon? I hope you have not gone hungry while I served you."

Soon after Chang had eaten, the chief hobbled into the teepee and said, "Please come and sit with us. We have things to discuss." Chang joined a small group of warriors sitting around a small fire in the center of the chief's section of the long lodge. Rolling Thunder sat next to the chief. Chang knew everyone present. Each one had been his teacher at one time or another.

Chief Looking Glass spoke, "My warriors say you have done well. You said you would stay for one moon, but you have been here two. You have learned much in two moons. I think it is time you leave us and continue your war with the Blackfoot. The season of the great cold and snows approaches. Our country does not get as cold as does the Blackfoot country. Their people have already moved into their lodges to keep warm near their fires. Now is a good time for you to fight them. It is not easy to pursue an enemy in the snow.

"Several times since you came to us the Blackfoot sent scouts to our camp. They have come in peace so we welcomed them. We told them why you were here. They think it is a good thing. They say it will make capturing you a greater challenge, like a coyote hunting a jackrabbit. The Blackfoot are pleased that you continue wearing the red cloth on your head. We thought it strange that you insisted on wearing it always, but now the Blackfoot know you are a man of honor.

"My people are the smallest band of the Nez Perce, but we are responsible to scout for the entire tribe. I always send scouts in pairs throughout the land. At least two of my scouts remain in the Blackfoot territory at all times. They also watch the white man closely. We want to know where they are digging and how many are in our land. The white men worry us very much. They don't just dig up the gold and leave, some of them stay and raise cattle or horses. We worry that soon there will be so many of them that they will chase us from our land. We don't want to fight them, but one day I think we must.

"My scouts also watch the Crow, the Cayuse, the Sioux, the Utes and even the white men at the salty lake. I sent word to Chief Joseph that the Sioux stole our horses. After that, the Sioux returned our horses, along with many of their horses in payment. Now we are no longer on the warpath with the Sioux.

"My scouts will know where you are, but they will not help you in your war, except to warn you of approaching danger. You must go now, but you are always welcome here among my people."

Chang asked, "How is your leg feeling chief."

"I must still take short steps, but my leg did not turn black. Now I know I will not die. Yellow Chief is a good medicine man." Chief Looking Glass lay on his sleeping robes and propped his injured foot up.

Rolling Thunder said, "You have learned more than we expected you would. There are many more things we could teach you, but that would take many more moons. You must go now because you can still travel over the pass. Soon the great snows will come and you will no longer be able to go that way.

"Now you speak with your hands you can talk to members of all tribes. You have learned how to hide your tracks and to follow those of others. You can conceal yourself almost anywhere, but most importantly, you have learned to put yourself in the head of your enemy so you can avoid him."

"Thank you," said Chang, "this means much to me."

"Gather up your things and get a buffalo robe to keep yourself warm. You should leave us in the morning. We will get your packhorses ready."

"Rolling Thunder," said Chang, "you are my friend. I wish to give the horses to you as a gift."

"Thank you Yellow Chief," the warrior smiled.

"Besides," said Chang, "I can travel more quickly without them."

"So," growled Rolling Thunder, the smile gone, "you are only giving me the horses because you don't want to take them with you."

"No," replied Chang, taken aback. "No, I really want you to have them."

Rolling Thunder roared with laughter, and patted Chang on the back. Chang sighed in relief.

It was well after daylight when Chang arose. He ate a good meal and thanked the chief for everything he had done. Chang put his gear on the horse then mounted it. He felt a chill in the air so he wrapped the buffalo robe around him. Chief Looking Glass and many other tribal members waved at Chang as he rode from the Nez Perce camp. He waved to them in return.

-EIGHT-

CHANG RODE SLOWLY up the Lolo Pass Trail, blanketed in snow. Snowdrifts kept pace with the altitude. The higher Chang went, the deeper the snowdrifts became. Soon the horse was pushing through waist high snow and several times the trek became so arduous that Chang had to dismount and lead the horse to blaze a trail through high drifts. He strayed from the path several times and had to double back to find it. It was backbreaking work and he removed the buffalo blanket to cool down. Before him, the mountain of snow seemed endless.

Only small patches of green from the pine trees relieved the sea of white. He struggled until his mind felt sluggish, and his muscles rebeled. It took all his willpower to keep one foot moving in front of the other. Darkness came unexpectedly. He was fortunate to find a decent area to camp before the night grew black. The ground was shielded by a think grove of trees, sufficient to provide protection from the snow provide small clusters of yellow grass for the horse to graze on. Chang unloaded the gear and turned the horse loose. Chang wrapped himself up in the buffalo skin and was asleep the minute he closed his eyes.

Chang awoke with a start early the next morning. He ached so badly he had trouble standing. He had a bite to eat and packed up for the second day of his journey over the pass. He thought the horse would be better if Chang walked, but he didn't have the strength. His only chance of getting off the mountain was to get back on the horse. If he didn't do it now, he might never have the strength to mount it again. Three times he tried to mount, and three times he failed. Summoning all his willpower, he took a mighty leap and dragged himself onto the horse's back.

After an hour, he wanted to give up. He wished he could lie down and sleep forever, but before him stood Morning Bird beckoning him. He felt no chill, but had enough presence of mind to keep bundled in the buffalo skin. The vision of his lover faded from view, but it gave him the desire to keep going. He must see Morning Bird again. It would not do to freeze to death on the mountain and never see her again—never explain to her what happened to him.

Chang glanced at the lead-colored sky. More snow was coming and he wondered how the Nez Perce had known that was probably the last day that the trail would be passable. His horse continued upward, staggering under the load. It stumbled several times. Almost imperceptibly, the incline leveled off in the afternoon. It took several minutes before Chang realized that the trail now sloped downward. "We passed the summit," he laughed giddily in the horse's ear. Although the trip was not over, the horse moved more quickly. At last, they rounded a sharp switchback and Chang was relieved to see the trail bottom out on the prairie below.

The snow seemed to disappear all at once. One minute the horse was slipping down the snow packed trail, and the next all traces of snow ahead were gone. It had been a hard trip from their camp to where he now stood. He knew the horse needed a breather, so he slid off its back. While they rested, Chang allowed the horse to graze. He was beginning to wonder if the horse would ever quit eating. It must have been famished.

Chang surveyed the land ahead. The valley was perhaps twenty miles across with a mountain range stretching from north to south on the far side. Chang checked the map Zeb had drawn. The main wagon road followed the base of the distant hills south past the Bannack Road turn-off, some forty miles away, and continued to Fort Hall beyond the Mormon settlement at the salty lake. After that, it continued south to

Mexico. Chang must find it to get to Bannack. He knew that Lost Trail Pass he had followed over a month ago would be snowbound now.

A few game trails etched in the snow ambled off in several directions but he saw no horse trails anywhere. He let the horse eat and rest for an hour then he remounted. Wrapping his buffalo robe more tightly around himself, he headed across the plains, grateful for the respite of the grueling trip over the pass. He gave the horse its head and he dozed off. He awoke to find the snow falling so heavily that he could only see a few feet ahead. He figured he had better stop before he lost his way. Besides, it was nearly dark. He found a deep gully offering protection from the wind and weather. He didn't feel hungry, but he knew he needed nourishment. After swallowing a few bites of food, he dug a small cave in the snow and settled in for the night. The snow cave was surprisingly warm and comfortable after the misery of the previous night. He watched the horse scrape through the snow with its hooves to find ample feed underneath.

The snowfall ebbed during the night, but was still coming down the following day as he traveling toward the foothills. The mountains were barely visible through the falling snow and knew he should be coming to the wagon road soon. He hoped he could find it in the snow. Dismounting, he led the horse as he watched for prairie dog holes. He knew if his horse stepped in one it could result in a broken leg. When they came atop a slight rise the horse alerted on something. Its nostrils flared as it caught the scent of something in the air, and its ears turned to lock onto a sound somewhere ahead. Then Chang saw the tracks of a large cat, probably a cougar. He pulled his rifle from the scabbard. As he continued, he came upon two large wagons standing side by side. Chang thought one of the wagons looked like a freight haulers. It appeared empty, but the other had a high canvas covering. The long wooden wagon tongues of both wagons were half snowed under.

Chang approached the wagons cautiously. He stopped abruptly and brought his rifle up to his shoulder when he saw a man standing near the front of the wagons. He was talking to someone inside the covered wagon. As Chang crept closer, he could see the man was an Indian and was speaking in a strange tongue. The Indian's horse stood several yards away. The Indian didn't appear to be threatening whoever was in the wagon, but was probably begging for food. Chang yelled to get the Indians attention, and with his rifle at the ready, he approached the wagon to investigate. He edged toward the back of the wagon and was startled when the canvas flap at the back opened and he found himself staring into the muzzle of a rifle held by a woman.

Chang froze. In a terrified voice, the woman screeched, "If you come any closer I'll shoot you dead, I will. You two go away and let us be. Haven't you hurt us enough? Get out of here now or I'll shoot!"

Chang lowered his gun, stepped back a few paces and said, "Put the gun down, ma'am, nobody's going to hurt you. I am here to help." The woman began to weave and she dropped the rifle. Her eyes rolled up in her head and she fainted backwards onto the floor of the wagon.

Chang called to the Indian at the front of the wagon who answered in some unintelligible language. Chang raised his hands and began communicating with hand signs. He learned the Indians name was Broken Tree, a Cayuse warrior from a small village about an hour east. He said he had come to warn the white people that a big snow was coming.

After opening the canvas flaps, Chang saw four people in the wagon. There were two young boys wrapped in quilts, huddled together to keep warm. The woman was sprawled across the body of a man who lay on his back. His bloody head protruded from a bundle of quilts. His nose angled to one side and several teeth lay near his head on the wagon bed. His body shuddered as he gasped for air.

Chang signaled Broken Tree to approach. The captain asked how they could help these people. As they communicated, a few flakes of snow fell and the wind picked up.

Chang told the two boys that a bad storm was coming and the Indian wanted them all to go to his warm lodge or they would freeze to death in the wagon. The two boys understood. They lifted the woman's head from the man. They patted her cheeks to rouse her. When she was alert enough, the boys told her what they had to do.

Broken Tree and Chang led their horses to the back of the wagon. After the boys helped the woman from the wagon, Chang and Broken Tree carried the unconscious man outside. They lay him belly down on Chang's horse and tied him on with a rope from the wagon. With assistance, the woman mounted the warrior's horse. Chang told the boys to follow the Indian closely and Chang would take up the rear.

The snow lay deep when at last the shivering group arrived at the Cayuse camp. Broken Tree yelled loudly in order to be heard above the howling wind. Several people exited the lodge and immediately helped the woman and man from the horses. They lay the man near a small fire in the center of the lodge.

Returning to the horse, Chang got his gear and tossed it through the flap of the lodge entrance. He followed the warrior as they led their horses to a sheltered area in a dense grove of trees. After he returned to Broken Tree's lodge, he saw Indian women cleaning the white man's face. The two boys sat quietly. Chang gathered his belongings and set them against the wall. He then sat cross-legged near the fire. He thanked the Indians for their assistance.

Much light filtered through the animal hide walls of the lodge. The hides had been scraped so thin they were translucent. He hadn't noticed this in the other lodges he had been in. Chang heard an Indian woman say something, and she sounded pleased. Then all the Indian women started chattering at the white woman. Chang knew they couldn't understand each other, but he could see the object of their pleasure. The white man had regained consciousness. He tried to sit up, but was unsuccessful. With the assistance of his wife, he was propped in a setting position. He tried to speak but winced in pain and reached for his mouth.

Chang smiled at the two boys and said, "I think your father is going to make it." The two boys grabbed each other's shoulders and looked into each other's eyes. They could hardly contain their excitement. Then curiosity overcame the Chinese man. "What were you doing out there in the wagons all alone?"

The boys' mother heard what Chang had asked and came over to kneel beside them saying, "It's so good to hear someone speak in English."

Chang asked, "Is this your entire family?"

The woman appeared to be in her early forties, with a slender build and medium height. She was dressed in a one piece, ground length grey woolen dress, buttoned tightly at the neck. Mussed light brown hair tinged with grey, and a tightly wrapped bun crowned her head. Pain and fatigue sculpted her narrow face. Chang wondered where she found the strength to care for her two sons and nurse her husband in the harsh surroundings around the covered wagon.

The wind howled as it battered the lodge. Chang knew that these people could never have survived the night with only their meager quilts and their God to keep them warm. He heard the woman earlier thank that God for taking Broken Tree and Chang to her wagon. The woman hugged her two boys and said, "I thank God for someone that speaks English. My name is Belle, Belle Thomas." She put her arms around one son and continued, "These are my sons, Jay, and Jim. My husband is Jake. He is a pastor of our church in St. Louis. We are missionaries that our God has chosen to become the pastor of a new church being built for us on the west coast near Portland. We came up the Missouri River to Fort Benton by steamboat. There we bought our two wagons and ten horses and planned to drive them to Fort Hall. After that we planned to head over the Blue Mountains to Portland. I drove one of our wagons and Jake drove the other."

"Unfortunately as you can see, we didn't make it. Indians attacked us several days ago. They took our horses and stole almost all we had. When Jake tried to stop them, one hit him in the face with a rifle butt and left him for dead. I was afraid they would rape and kill me, but it was too cold. They just took all they could carry and left us there. I thought Jake would die and I could do nothing for him. I hoped someone would come to help us, but I had about lost hope. I prayed for the lives of my boys and God answered my prayers by sending you to rescue us. God is truly wonderful."

"I think your husband will survive," said Chang. "He appears to be very strong. Your boys are very brave. They must have given you much in help taking care of your husband. You should be very proud of them."

The woman looked at her two sons and smiled, "I am," she said.

"My name is Chang. I live in the town of Bannack about forty miles south of here. I was trying to find the wagon road that leads there when I came across wagons. Broken Tree was searching for you because the Crow Indians who stole your horses told him what they had done. He knew you could not survive the blizzard he knew was coming. You owe your lives to him not me."

A blast of icy wind whipped through the lodge as the entrance flap opened and several Indians came in. They brushed snow from their clothing and stood before the fire to warm themselves. One was Broken Tree. He told Chang in the hand language that the two men accompanying him spoke English, so they could all talk to the white people.

The three warriors sat before the fire. One of the newcomers said, "I am Chief Good Water of this band of Cayuse tribe. Many Crow come to our camp and tell us they take the horses of some white people riding in big tents on wheels. They tell us of a white woman and her boys. They tell us they kill the white man and all would soon freeze. He say the coyote will eat the white people.

"My warrior Broken Tree is brother to the white people. Many moons ago some white people came to the land of the Cayuse and Nez Perce to tell us of the great spirit in the sky. The family of Broken Tree was very sick and the white man made them well. Broken Tree want to save lives of these white people so the great sky spirit will continue to keep his family from harm. Broken Tree does not speak the tongue of the white people or the tongue of the yellow people yet he says he can hand talk with you. I have never seen a yellow man who could speak the hand language. Where did you learn this?"

Chang replied, "I learned to hand talk from the Nez Perce. I have just come from the Nez Perce village of Chief Looking Glass. He is a good friend."

Chief Good Water said, "One of my women is the daughter of Chief Looking Glass. The Cayuse and Nez Perce have always been good friends. You were lucky to pass through the high snow on Lolo Trail. This is not a good time to ride in the mountains. It would be wise to stay here in our village until the great snows stop. You will be warm in one of our lodges and we will give you something to eat until you can travel again."

Chang thought about this for a moment then replied, "I am very happy to be here in your warm lodge and I thank you for your hospitality. I wousld have to live in a cave in the snow until the snows cease if I hadn't came here with your warrior, Broken Tree. To repay your hospitality, when I can travel through the snow again, I will go to the town of Bannack where I have many trading things. Send warriors with me I will fill send them with many fine things for your women. I will also give you gunpowder and sharp knives to repay you and your people. I also hope to pay you for these white people's horses. Perhaps you can buy them or steal them back from the Crow."

Belle interrupted, "Why do you want to help us? We are strangers to you. We are only God's missionaries. That means nothing to you."

Chang replied, "Wouldn't you help me or my people if you found us in trouble like you are? Of course you would. Your God doesn't care what color his people are. He made us all and only painted our skin so we know where we came from."

Chief Good Water said, "Our cousins, the Blackfoot sent scouts to our village several times in the last two moons to visit us. The Blackfoot, the Crow, the Sioux all asked us if we see a yellow man they call the Yellow Chief. They say he wears a red cloth on his head, like the one your wear. The Blackfoot say they would give many horses to their brothers, the Cayuse, if we will catch this yellow man and give him to them. Have you heard this story? Are you the Yellow Chief?"

Chang removed the red headband and said, "Yes, I am Yellow Chief. Would you like to hear my story?"

"Sitting next to a fire while the snows fall is a good time for a story." The chief sent for warriors from some of the other lodges to come and hear the story. Many came, and when the lodge was full the chief signaled for quiet, then he said, "Tell us Yellow Chief how you came to our Cayuse village."

So that all could understand, Chang spoke simultaneously in English and in the Indian hand language. The story lasted several hours because people kept asking questions to learn more details about certain points. Chang told of his experiences with the Blackfoot, in the town of Bannack, and of going to the Nez Perce tribe to learn the way of the Indian. Finishing his story at last, Chang looked around at the group in the lodge and added, "I told you of my war with the Blackfoot. I have no desire to kill more of them, but they say if I don't fight them until they hang my scalp from their scalp pole they will kill many more of my Chinese brothers. My brothers' lives are worth more than my own."

Chief Good Water looked around at his people crowded up in the small lodge. He told them, "The Blackfoot tell us why they are at war with the Yellow Chief and now we have heard from the yellow man why he fights the Blackfoot. You and the Blackfoot speak the same words, it is a matter of honor for them to hunt you down and cut off your scalp.

"The Cayuse are not at war with the Blackfoot so we will not fight them. I will help you any other way I can, but my warriors must speak for themselves. Perhaps one among us will sell you to the Blackfoot for a horse, but if he does he is not welcome to ride his new horse in my village."

There was a murmur from the crowd then one of the warriors stood and said, "The Yellow Chief is safe in our village. We will watch his war with the Blackfoot and hope he lives so he can come back and continue his story."

Belle spoke up, "Why do you have to fight them? Can't you talk to each other to settle your differences?"

"I wish it was that easy," Chang replied, "but I think it will only end when they have my scalp."

Belle's jaw began to quiver so Chang quickly added, "How is your husband? He's very lucky to still be alive."

"He is doing much better."

"You will be safe here with the Cayuse until your husband is well enough to travel. I will send trade goods back here to Chief Good Water so he can buy horses to pull your wagons to Bannack. I don't know what kind of work you or Jake can do, but you won't have any trouble finding some way to make enough money in Bannack to get you to Portland."

"My husband is a skilled carpenter. I'm sure God will help us. I'm a school teacher, but I doubt they need a teacher in a wild mining town. People say I'm a pretty good cook though."

Chang looked at her husband's ample belly and said, "I'll bet you are. Belle, if you are a teacher, maybe you could teach these people to speak English. It will give you something to do until your husband heals."

"I will," she promised.

Noticing several rifles leaning against the wall, Chang picked one up and sat by the fire to examine it. He asked the chief, "This is one of those new American army rifles. It is a top-loading Sharps, the best rifle their army has. How did you manage to get these?"

Chief Good Water said, "We traded horses to the blue coats for these guns. They are very good guns but almost useless to us. We trade one horse for one rifle and one horse for five bullets but no more. They tell us the big chief of the blue coat army say this is enough to kill five deer. We have many of these fine rifles but have no bullets. We can't reload them like we do our other guns by putting gunpowder in the barrel. The blue coats maybe think we shoot at them if we have many bullets."

Chang asked him, "Do you still have the empty cartridges you shot?"

The chief tossed him an empty cartridge and said, "We have many of these useless bullets. The blue coats give them to our women to wear around their necks and for our children to play with, but they won't trade us bullets we can shoot."

Chang looked the empty cartridge over and said, "My people in Bannack make gunpowder we use in the gold mines to blow rocks out of the streams or to load guns. They also know how to reload these cartridges. They showed me how to do it so I could reload my own bullets. I can show you how to reload these empty cartridges."

The chief said, "This will save my people many horses. Most of my warriors have one of these guns but they are saving bullets to shoot buffalo after the big snows. We could kill more deer and bear to eat if we used this new gun to hunt."

Chang drew his knife from the scabbard hanging on his back and punched a small hole at the back of the cartridge casing. He twisted the knife to enlarge the hole and asked the chief for one of the percussion caps, used in the muskets. When the hole was the right size for the cap to fit snuggly in the hole, he split the sides of the cap near the top and pushed it into the hole. He bent the split sides tightly against the back of the case to secure it. He told the chief, "Now we fill it with gunpowder and put the lead bullet in the end. I'll need one of your musket balls and gunpowder." Chief Good Water handed over the items. Chang was pleased that the musket balls were slightly larger than the fifty-caliber Sharps rifle bullet.

Chang took the wooden stick he had used to press the split cap into the case. He then measured the length of the case with the stick and made a mark on it exactly half way. "We must fill the case exactly half full of gunpowder. Do not use too much powder or the gun might blow up. If you do not use enough the lead bullet might stick in the barrel." When the cartridge was half-full, he took the lead ball and forced it into the open end. The pliant musket ball slowly formed to the exact size of the cartridge casing. When the lead was even with the casing he tossed the reloaded cartridge to the chief and said, "Put it in your rifle and see if it shoots."

Chief Good Water loaded the cartridge in his rifle and stepped out in the snowstorm. He pointed the rifle skyward and pulled the trigger. The sound of the rifle crack echoed through the lodge. When the chief returned inside, he smiled and said. "It works. It is fine thing you taught me. My people will be happy. Now we use these fine rifles for hunting all meat, not just the buffalo. Please show my warriors how you do this."

Chang replied, "Chief Good Water, I do not wish to offend you or your fine warriors, but I should show your women how to reload these bullet for you. Your women are used to doing small work with their hands. They sew beads and moccasins. These bullets must all be made exactly alike. It is long and tedious work to make many. Your warriors will make many mistakes."

The chief said, "Perhaps you are right. My warriors may think that more powder will make the bullets shoot farther." The storm continued for several days as Chang showed the women how to reload bullets. It pleased Chang when he heard the rifle fire as warriors tested the bullets made by the women.

One morning Chang awoke to silence. The wind had blown so long that the stillness seemed almost eerie. He roused himself from his warm buffalo robe, pushed the lodge entrance flap aside and stepped outside into snow piled high on the ground. He squinted in the dazzling sunlight. It seemed the landscape was ablaze with white light. The clustered teepees pointed toward a sky of radiant blue. Tribal members from all over camp emerged from their teepees and called greetings to one another. Children spilled out of lodges to frolic in the snow. Smiles greeted him everywhere. Chang felt empty. He was going to miss these people.

Later in the day, Chang told the chief, "It is time for me to leave. I will start for Bannack in the morning. If you will send three or four of your warriors with me I will get some trade goods for them to bring back here for you and to help the Thomas family."

Chang headed out early the next morning. Late that afternoon he and four of Chief Good Water's warriors trudged through waist high snow, following the wagon road south toward Bannack. Chang was glad these Indians were traveling with him as they could alternate taking the front to break trail for the others. Coming into a narrow, deep canyon, the Indians veered off the road and climbed the canyon wall a short distance. Chang followed. They arrived at a deep overhang free of snow. They gathered dry brush and soon had a welcome fire blazing. They warmed themselves, ate jerky strips, wrapped up in their blankets and were immediately asleep.

The sun helped melt the snow the following day. Although the snow was still deep, it became increasingly manageable to pass through. Shortly after noon, they stood on a hill and looked down upon the town of Bannack. They could see many columns of smoke drifting up from the chimneys of shacks, houses, lean-tos, dugouts and anything else offering shelter. The streets and creek were devoid of people. Chang and the warriors continued their trip toward town. They circled around behind the tong house, where Chang put the horses in the barn. After caring for and feeding the horses, he led the four warriors through the backdoor. Chang told them to wait in the kitchen while he spoke to the tong. Zing Yong was seated at his desk and Chang coughed to catch his attention. The tong saw Chang, leapt from his chair and shook Chang's hand. Zing Yong exclaimed, "So our Yellow Chief has returned!"

-NINE-

PLEASED AT THE exuberant greeting, Chang said, "It's so good to see you again, I hope your family is well.

"I have four Indians with me. May they stay the night?"

"Of course they may stay," Zing Yong replied. "I'll get my cooks to make us something to eat, you're probably hungry."

Chang chuckled at the diametric sight as Zing Yong bounced into the room ahead of him to greet the Indians. Zing Yong was dressed in a thick pleated silk black shirt buttoned tightly around the neck, which seemed to squeeze his round head into a ball. Black pleated trousers of the same material covered his short legs, giving him the appearance of a black snowman. Each of the Indians, on the other hand, wore a leather suit and moccasins, complemented by a tight fitting animal skin hat draped behind his head. The hats covered the Indian's ears and necks. The Indians all had thick, soft buffalo skin blankets wrapped around their upper bodies.

Chang introduced the Indians, "These warriors are my new Cayuse friends who will stay with us tonight." Then pointing to Zing Yong he said, "This is our Chinese Chief, Zing Yong. This is his lodge and he welcomes you. I'll show you where we sleep while he gets us something to eat." Chang then led the warriors upstairs to the dormitory.

A few minutes later Zing Yong came in and said, "The food is ready. Let us eat while you update me on what you have been doing."

Chang noticed how awkward the Indians seemed sitting in chairs. They stared at the tableware as if they had no idea how to use it. Zing Yong noticed their discomfort and said, "Eat in any manner most comfortable to you." Still they hesitated. Chang pulled out his knife, stabbed a large venison steak and began to eat with his fingers. The Indians smiled, grabbed the venison with their hands, stuffed it in their mouths and chomped on it noisily.

Zing Yong sighed. He laid his silverware on the table and followed suit. With grease running down his cheek he asked, "Tell me what you have been doing Captain Chang."

Chang told all that had occurred since leaving the tong house. Chang then told of his promise to send trade goods to the Cayuse chief. "I have enough money in my account with you to buy enough items to load two pack horses and send them back with these warriors. With your help I can send them on their way in the morning."

Zing Yong replied, "I'll get the trade goods you want. If the missionaries can pay me back they may, but they do not need to. You do not need to pay for the trade goods. You will need your money to fight the Blackfoot. If your Cayuse friends don't mind, I would like to bring my family over here to meet them this evening."

The Cayuse warriors chosen to accompany Chang all spoke English. They were listening to the conversation and one asked, "We would like to meet your family. How many women do you have?"

Zing Yong laughed and said, "Three, but two are daughters. I only have one wife. She keeps me busy enough. I also have a fine young son. You should stay in the tong house while you are in Bannack. Many miners are drunk most of the time right now because they cannot work their mines in the snow. You never know what they might do when they get drunk."

Chang decided he would stay here with them too. He didn't want the merchants to notice him buying Indian trade goods. As tong, Zing Yong would not attract attention for buying a great deal of merchandise. It was getting dark whey they finished packing up the trade goods Zing Yong had obtained. The warriors expected a small bag or two of beads and gunpowder, but when the tong handed them two overloaded packs of cloth, thread, needles, and cap and ball repeating pistols, their eyes bulged. Chang knew that four pistols would be gone from the packs before the warriors got out of Bannack.

That evening, Zing Yong entered the tong house with his family. Chang set out some chairs in a half circle for the tong's family, but the four Indians preferred to sit cross-legged on the floor. Zing Yong introduced his family then asked the Indians their names. The first of the four thumped himself on his chest and said in a low guttural voice, "I am called Star Gettas. That means Burnt Grass in English. I have two wives, one is Nez Perce and one is Sioux. I have three sons who will soon become brave Cayuse warriors." The other three Indians introduced themselves in turn. Each one had a family of which he was proud.

Chang explained to the tong's family how the Cayuse had saved the lives of the missionaries, the Thomas family. He also said that the four warriors had came to get the trade goods Chang had promised them to trade for horses to pull the Thomas' wagons. He continued, "All the Cayuse horses are hunting or warhorses. They are not trained to pull wagons. I hope I am giving enough trade goods for the Thomas family to buy new horses. The Cayuse tribe is giving them lodging and helping Jake, the wounded man, to recover.

The warriors were pleased to learn that Zing Yong's wife, Starlight, was an Indian from the Cheyenne tribe. Zing Yong's family was interested to learn how the Cayuse got along with the other tribes in the area and with the white men invading their country. While they were talking, Zing Yong slipped out and returned with a large cake the women had made for the occasion. Starlight cut large pieces and put them on glass plates, each with an accompanying fork. After serving everyone, she watched in amusement as the Indians looked at it, shrugged and used their fingers to stuff the cake in their mouths. They chewed with obvious pleasure, belched loudly and nodded in appreciation. She learned that the only sweets they usually ate were made of honey, when they were lucky enough to find beehives. She cut the rest of the cake into four large pieces, gave each warrior a piece and they devoured them instantly.

All too soon for Chang, Zing Yong stood and said, "It's getting late and these men need sleep if they are leaving at daylight." Chang's heart pounded as Morning Bird's eyes met his and they said goodbye once again.

Zing Yong picked two of his worst horses, knowing he would never get them back. He then tied on the packs. Before the Indians mounted their riding horses, the tong told them, "There are problems with some of the white men in the area. They rob people of everything. Quite often, they kill from ambush before robbing them. I do not think you will be noticed leaving town this early in the morning, but be careful."

Burnt Grass said, "Thank you for the warning. One of us will ride ahead and one behind the packhorses as a precaution." The Indians mounted the horses as Chang opened the corral gate. The riders bid farewell as they rode into the cold morning breeze.

Zing Yong led Chang back to office and said, "Be mighty careful here, some Indians have been in town asking about the Chinaman with a red cloth on his head."

"Thanks for telling me," Chang replied. "What about those bandits?"

"We don't know much about them, but there are several, and they are well organized. In the past month, nearly every stagecoach leaving Bannack and Virginia City was held up. I have not sent any of our gold to San Francisco in over two months so none of ours is lost yet. I hope to convince the robbers we do not have gold worth stealing, yet they hold up even empty stagecoaches. If they knew the amount gold hidden in the tong house they would tear it to pieces. I wonder if Sheriff Plummer is involved."

"Why do you say that?"

"He is a silver-tongued politician for the entire territory round about. He fooled everyone with a false story of where he came from. Our people checked him out and we're sure he's not who he pretends to be."

"Between the bandits and the Blackfoot, I may have trouble getting out of town. The Blackfoot probably know I am here in Bannack. I need to stay alive while I gather the supplies I need. Do our people still make gun powder in the powder house in the hill?"

"Yes, making blasting powder has become a very profitable business for us. Fortunately, we have some expert black powder makers. They found a large cave nearby that is the home for millions of bats. Bat dung or guano is the richest source of nitrate there is. They also located ample supplies of sulfur near the volcanic activities in the Yellowstone country just east of here and we make charcoal from some of the trees nearby. Mining our own nitrate, saltpeter, sulfur and charcoal, we make black powder for firearms, although most is used as blasting powder. We build small waterproof wooden kegs that hold five pounds of blasting powder, perfect for blowing one hundred pound rocks from the creek bottom."

Chang replied, "I could use some powder in smaller containers. I will speak with the powder makers tomorrow to find out what they can do for me. I need to get some things in town today but I want to leave here in six days so I can set up around the Blackfoot camp at the full moon."

"Why?"

"To play on their superstitions."

Late that afternoon Chang went in to Hassler's Mercantile and Mining Supply owned by the Bannack town mayor. At the rear of the store at a large firearms display, he was surprised to find a long-barreled Hawkins muzzleloader like the one Zeb loaned him. As he was examining the rifle, Mr. Hassler the proprietor said, "That's a real nice rifle there. Sell it to you cheap. Not much call for muzzle loaders no more. Everybody wants a repeater. Hey, are you that Chinaman the Indians keep asking about? I see the red cloth on your head."

"Yes," Chang answered.

"They wouldn't tell me why they were interested in you."

Chang asked, "When was the last time you saw one of these Indians?"

"Why," Mr. Hassler answered, "Just a few minutes ago. Fact is, he is getting on that horse across the street right now."

Tossing the rifle to the clerk Chang said, "Hang onto this gun, I'll be right back. I need to talk to him." He sprinted across the street, yelling at the Indian as he started to ride off. The Indian turned and when he recognized Chang he raised his rifle. Chang yelled, "Put that gun down! I want to talk to you."

The Indian hesitated and when several white men approached, he lowered his gun. Chang said, "You have been looking for me, the Yellow Chief, and now you found me. Go back to your village and tell Chief Three Fingers, that I am coming for his scalp at the full moon. Tell him that every time he sees a coyote in the grass or a cat in the rocks it might be me coming to get his scalp. Tell your chief that your women and children will go hungry and he will not sleep well at night until we settle this war. The scalp of Chief Three Fingers will hang from my scalp pole if he does not call off this war with the Yellow Chief."

The Indian, half sneeringly, grated, "I'll tell my chief what you say." Viciously kicking his horse in the flanks, he galloped out of town.

Chang returned to the store and picked up the rifle he had been looking at. Mr. Hassler asked, "What did you tell him? He sure left town in a hurry."

"Just a misunderstanding," Chang replied. He looked at several cartridge pistols. One was a .45 caliber like the one he already had, but with a much shorter barrel. It wouldn't be as accurate at a distance, but he could carry it concealed in the pocket of his jacket easily. He bought both the rifle and the pistol. Chang picked up caps for the rifle. Mr. Hassler tossed a box of cartridges for the pistol on the counter. "Here. They're for your new pistol. They're on the house."

When Chang got back to the tong house he told Zing Yong of his encounter with the Blackfoot scout. Seeing the muzzle-loading rifle, Zing Yong asked, "Is there something wrong with your repeater? It shoots faster than the muzzleloader."

"The repeater works just fine," Chang replied, "but I want this one for its long range and accuracy. I've got everything I need from town for now, but I would like to meet with your powder makers about those other items."

Zing Yong replied, "I spoke to them already. They are anxious to meet you and show you what they have. I'll take you there tomorrow."

"Good."

"Then it is set. Would you like to come to dinner again tonight?"

"Yes, sir," Chang perked up.

"You know the place and time."

After knocking on the door of Zing Yong's house, Chang was elated when Morning Bird invited him in with a white, toothy smile. She led him into the sitting room and said, "It's so good to see you again Captain Chang. I hope your business up north went well. My father says you will be here for a few days then you are going out of town." She gazed expectantly at Chang.

The captain took Morning Bird's hand in his; the touch was electrifying. Her soft warm hand in his was so natural, he felt as if he were home. They sat in a comfortable silence until Zing Yong entered the room. When he saw the two of them, he said, "So here you are. You two better come and eat, or there will be a lot of wasted food."

After dinner, Morning Bird said, "When talking and visiting with my friends I heard that there are some Indians that come to Bannack quite often seeking a Chinese person who wears a red headband. What do they want?"

Taken aback, Chang had to think for a moment on how to answer. He didn't want to tell her of his problem with the Blackfoot but he couldn't outright lie to her either. "The Indians are from a Blackfoot village south of here. We had a small disagreement sometime back but I can straighten it out. I am going to their camp next week to talk to them about it." Chang thought Morning Bird's eyes flashed doubt.

The tong, quickly changing the subject, said, "I just heard that several white men had a fight with a few Indians on the road going north from town. The Indians may have been our friends, the Cayuse. Nobody was killed but one white man was wounded in the leg. Marshal Fielding put him in jail to await trial. The townsfolk think the white men are the road agents who have been doing so many holdups hereabouts. The wounded man isn't getting much sympathy from the locals."

Chang replied, "It is a good thing you warned the warriors of the possibility of ambush."

After a little more conversation about the bandits the tong asked, "Have you given any thought of what you will do when you have finished the business your general sent you over here to do?"

"I am a captain in my general's army, so I must go where he sends me. Still, I believe this is where I belong."

"I send reports to the general and your father each month concerning our affairs here. In return, your father sends me a brief report of happenings in China. Some of the news is very disturbing. As you know, the Emperor of China is Tong Zhi, the boy emperor they call him. Everyone knows it is his mother Ci Xi who rules the nation. Foreigners, Europeans mostly, influence her. They want to exploit

China's great resources to their own advantage. For a few gifts and many promises, they convinced her that she should be in charge of the Chinese military. They say she should assign governors to provinces and territories—people loyal to her of course.

"Recently she conscripted most of the military forces of Governor-General Zeng Gudean into the national Chinese Army. Zeng Gudean may be removed from power. Your father fears that as the Chinese peasants lose the protection of their local warlords and see their taxes raised far beyond what they can pay, there is going to be a rebellion. It could lead to a blood bath that will tear China apart for generations. Your father Li Wong and most of the existing warlords inquired about accommodations here in America if they must flee China in exile. He wants to know about business opportunities in America, particularly for maritime shipping. I know little about that, so I referred him to our tong in San Francisco. I sent information on a new steam propelled river boat though."

Chang was astonished at the recent events in China. He wouldn't serve in a national emperor's army. His lifelong plan of a military career was gone in a snap. Now instead of rejoining his family in China, it might be joining him in America. The importance of Chang's current mission suddenly seemed miniscule. Nevertheless, the fact that Chang was in America might prove valuable for his family and General Zeng Gudean. Chang said, "I already considered staying in America because of you and your beautiful daughter Morning Bird. Now that I know of the developments in China, I am sure I would like to stay here. Honorable Tong Zing Yong, if I remain I would like your permission to court Morning Bird."

Chang felt Morning Bird stiffen. Blushing, she looked deep into his eyes as if searching his very soul. She gently squeezed his hand in hers and looked away. Zing Yong looked at the pair for two or three minutes. Making a decision, he said, "I live in America and I plan to stay here. That makes me an American and Americans do as they please. I can't and won't make that decision for her. I won't decide who courts and marries my daughters."

-    -   -

The Chinese gunpowder factory was only about a half mile from the tong house. It was an easy walk, but he wanted to exercise his horse so he mounted up and rode over the hill. Stopping at the top, he had a good view of the town and the gold mines in the creek below. A warm breeze ruffled the hair exposed above the headband. Swift torrents of muddy water from the melting snow flowed in every gully and ravine toward Rattlesnake Creek, which had overrun its banks. Unlike the day of his return, the town was now alive with hundreds of miners moving their mining equipment to higher ground. Due to the heavy traffic on Main Street, it was a sea of knee-high mud. The ground most everywhere else was more firm. Several large wagons were stuck axle deep in the mud in the road. Many people slopped around in the muck trying to move the wagons out of the way.

Chang urged his mount downhill toward the powder works. Several uniformly built homes sat in one side of a road and a group of large buildings were on the other. Huge piles of materials were stacked around the buildings but the powder factory itself was inside the hill. The Chinese had built several huge rooms in the manmade cave and boarded up the opening except for one large door at the entrance. The door was large enough for a freight wagon to back into the cave. The intent of building the powder works in a cave was to save the town in the event of an explosion.

Chang rode to the entrance of the underground facility. As he dismounted, a huge man met him and led the horse to a hitching post. The man looped the lead rope around the post and said, "You must be Chang. Zing Yong told me you were coming. Come inside and we'll talk."

Wooden beams braced against the floor supported the roof. Chang saw fifteen or twenty people busy at work. As the two men entered a small office built against one wall, the large man sat and motioned for Chang to do the same. The man said, "I'm Sammy Zong, I run this place. I did most of the work myself until last year. Business is booming," he laughed at his own pun. "I've got so much work now that we had to hire more help. We ship about two tons of explosives every day. The miners have learned it's a lot easier to blow rocks out of the way than to pack them out."

Chang nodded politely but said nothing. The man continued, "The tong tells me you have something in mind. What can we do for you?"

"Did Zing Yong tell you of my war with the Blackfoot?"

"A little, yes."

Chang told him of his ideas to keep the Indians on edge with miniature powder bombs. "If I can make life miserable for them they might call the war off, at least that is what I hope." Do you know anything about making fireworks? They, along with the small bombs, might help frighten the Indians, especially if I get there in time for the full moon."

"I'm the best fireworks maker in the world. I just started making up some to put on a show here in Bannack on the Fourth of July."

"Great," said Chang. For the next several days, Chang rode over to help Sammy Yong build small rockets. The biggest challenge was rolling paper into tubes to hold the rocket propellant, and not having it leak.

Soon there were dozens of small powder bombs made up. They were square waterproof wooden boxes about six inches across. They were easy to stack and transport on a packhorse. Each box could bring down a teepee. Sammy showed Chang a set of waterproof fuses and said, "Be careful when you light these, they flame up brightly and release plenty of smoke. Someone might see you lighting them in the day or the night. If you can't hide the fuses, cover them with something while they burn."

Chang replied, "I know it takes a spark or flame to explode the gunpowder, but suppose I put some percussion caps in with the powder then shoot the powder box. I think a bullet would explode one of these caps and set off the powder."

"Yes," Sammy said, "That would work. Even a bullet hitting the box would be enough to explode the caps. I can use that idea at a fireworks show. A sharpshooter could set off a powder keg from a distance. My men wouldn't have to light a fuse then run like hell to escape. Speaking of fuses, I've marked these I made for you. They have one, five and ten minute burn times."

Mounting his little warhorse, Chang rode around the hill to the main road just as he had the past several days. It was longer, but a lot easier than riding over the top of the hill. As he rode into the outskirts of Bannack his horse flinched, jerked erect and crumpled over on its side. It came to rest on Chang's leg. Bright red blood gushed from the horse's neck where it had been shot. Chang pushed himself from under his downed horse just as the crack of another gunshot rang out. Frantically he searched for the source of the gunshot. He rose on his knees and another bullet thumped the horse's carcass. There were at least two shooters, firing from different places. He spotted one across the street behind a wagon, but was unsure where the second was. Then Chang spotted him. The head of a Blackfoot warrior popped up from the roof of a shanty down the street. A bullet impacted the mud in front of his face, splashing blinding morass into his eyes.

He wiped his eyes, but only had limited success in restoring his vision. He could barely see. Cursing himself for leaving his rifle in the tong house, he withdrew the pistol from his pocket, pointed it in the general direction of the Indian on the roof, and pulled the trigger. There was only a dull click. The gun was empty. He had forgotten to load it. Jerking the box of cartridges out of his pocket and tearing it open, he dropped most of the cartridges on the ground as he frantically tried to push a cartridge into a chamber. It wouldn't fit—it was the wrong caliber.

Thrusting the pistol back in his pocket he stood to run, but lost his footing and sprawled on the ground. Several more bullets hit the ground around him as he got to his feet and sprinted toward the shanty. He zigzagged while running, but an agonizing blow to his right hip knocked him down again. While still rolling from the momentum of his run, he launched himself back to his feet and hobbled through the door of the shanty. As he dove inside, two men dressed only in long underwear, leapt past him and ran hollering up the street.

Chang rubbed his eyes again, regaining a little more of his vision. He looked about, but saw no other doors from the shanty. A pistol hung in a holster on the back of a rickety chair. Chang grabbed the gun and fired the percussion-cap revolver three times through the roof, then moved out of the way to avoid return fire. A fraction of a second later a bullet fired from atop the roof struck exactly where he had been standing. A scuffling noise on the roof followed, and the Indian jumped from the roof and ran toward the other bushwhacker behind the wagon. Chang smashed the glass from a window, and fired two rounds. He saw the Indian stagger then regain his balance. Chang took careful aim and squeezed the trigger but the gun was empty. Chang threw a chair through a rear window and dove through the opening. He hobbled down the street, keeping the shack between himself and the ambushers. As he jogged past a saloon, the front porch was crowded with spectators who yelled and cheered him on.

As he ran, his hip grew more painful. He headed to the tong house and arrived there without further gunfire. He grabbed his repeating rifle and was about to go after the Indians when his leg gave way. Reeling with pain, he opened his trousers expecting to see a bloody wound. Instead, a large welt covered his hip. He pulled the pistol from his pocket and saw that one side of the wooden handgrip was shattered where a bullet struck it. He smiled in relief—he was not wounded after all. He refastened his pants and hobbled out the backdoor toward the wagon where he had last seen the Indians, but he was too late. They were riding over the hill, one Indian supported on his horse by the other.

After a sleepless pain-filled night, morning found Chang packing a horse borrowed from the tong. After he loaded all the items he was taking with him, he tried to mount the steed, but he couldn't bend his hip. "Better use a ladder," a voice behind him said. It was Morning Bird. At any other time, her voice would have been a welcome euphony—not this morning. Chang did not look around. "I wish you had not come," he said. He couldn't take this right now.

"I thought you told me the Indians weren't trying to harm you."

"That is not exactly what I said."

"But it's what you led me to believe. Everyone in town is talking about your battle with the Blackfoot. They say you are fighting the entire tribe, not just one or two Indians."

"Morning Bird, I..."

"Yet you speak to me of spending our lives together. How long a life will you have? Months, days, hours? Why was I the last to know of this—this war? If you really meant what you told father, if you really meant to court me, I should have been the first to know of this war, not the last." Chang still did not turn around, even when he heard the barn door slam. Chang had to stand on a box before he could mount the horse. He rode slowly, pain streaking up his side with each step of the horse, as he led two packhorses over the hill to the powder factory.

-TEN-

LTHOUGH CHANG EXAMINED every riding horse in the tong's barn, he had been unable to find a suitable one. All of the tong's horses needed bridles and reins to control them. For an Indian war, he thought, I need an Indian horse. The only way I can get one quickly is to steal one from the Blackfoot. That became his plan. He took the tong's horse for now, fully intending to send it home as soon as he could find an Indian-trained appaloosa.

At the gunpowder factory, he slid painfully off the back of the horse then tied all the horses to the hitching rail. Sammy called to him, "Well Chang, it looks like you're getting serious about fighting those redskins. Come on inside and I'll show you what I have prepared. He opened the door and they entered the cave building. Against one wall were several small powder boxes. Each box had lacquer waterproofing and a small hole drilled in one side for a fuse. Every five boxes were tied together into bundles for easy loading and unloading. Chang commented, "Zing Yong said you were a master at making and packing explosives, and I can see why. This is perfect for what I need, small and easy to transport. They are worth anything you wish to charge me."

Sammy smiled and said, "No charge for these. If you can help our Chinese people, we should pay you. Besides, if your idea of putting percussion caps in the powder boxes works, it will save many Chinese lives. Come over here and look at these rockets. Suspended from the ceiling were about 30 long slender cylindrical objects. Each was about three inches in diameter and twenty inches in length, with a cone-shaped tip fastened at one end and a long fuse extending from the other. The fuse of each rocket wrapped around the cylinder. Chang assumed that the fuse was long to give the person lighting it plenty of time to move away before it ignited the rocket. He knew he could shorten the launch time easily enough by clipping off part of the fuse. "The rockets are beautiful Sammy. Do they display different colors when they explode?"

Sammy answered, "I've hit a snag there. The bright flashes of light happen when shavings of metal ignite and blow away from the rocket during the explosion. The light bursts are intense, but about the only metal I have available right now is iron. Iron only produces white light. I'm trying to find other metals to make red and green flashes, but I haven't found the right materials yet. Let's take a couple of bombs and rockets outside and I'll show you how they work. Do you have that rifle with you to ignite the bombs?"

"It is in the scabbard on my horse."

The men took two rockets and two bombs outside. Chang retrieved his rifle and reloading materials from the horse, and the two men walked a short distance up the hill. Sammy set one of the bombs on a rock about 200 yards away. When he returned to Chang's position he said, "Let's see if that idea for igniting powder with your rifle works." Chang sat, propped his rifle on a rock, sighted and squeezed the trigger. A huge blast erupted.

"It works, it works," laughed Sammy, the enormous man danced around giddily like a child with a new toy. "You were right, the percussion caps set it off, but only because you are such a good marksman."

Picking up the other powder container and forcing a short length of fuse into the hole on the side of the box, Sammy said, "It burns at about sixty seconds per foot." Chang took the powder box to the same area where the last box exploded. He didn't think he needed a full minute to escape the blast, so he cut the fuse short and lit it with a new wooden matchstick Sammy gave him. Chang was so excited about the explosives that he forgot that his hip wasn't working right. As he turned to run, the pain in his hip shot through his body and he fell to the ground.

He barely had presence of mind enough to cover his ears before the explosive device covered him with pebbles and dirt.

When Chang limped back to Sammy's location, the larger man joked, "That was mighty impressive running for a little guy." Then more seriously, he asked, "Are you hurt?"

"Just my pride," Chang answered.

"In the future, don't cut them so short. Give yourself time to get away."

"I will try to remember that."

Sammy grinned. "Most of the fuses should burn about three minutes. I plugged the fuse holes in the bombs to help make them waterproof like the powder kegs the miners use in the stream. Of course, you will have to light the fuse before you put the bomb in the water. At any rate, I'm pleased with the bombs. They work better than I expected them to."

"I'm happy with them too," said Chang. "They are small, light and loud. They are just what I wanted."

"We have many ingenious people working here. One of them is Jo Jong, a real fireworks artist. He came up with a simple way for us to make rocket bodies. He took a large paper sign from the front of one of the hardware stores. He discovered that he can roll the paper up into any size to make the fireworks rocket bodies. It will make about fifty of various sizes."

"Wasn't he afraid of being caught stealing it? Those miners can get pretty mean."

"Oh, he didn't steal it. He said he would paint the front of Mr. Hassler's store in trade."

"I'm glad; I wouldn't want any of our people in trouble with the law."

"Jo Jong also discovered that by putting six independent charges under the conical end of the rocket, when the propellant power burns to the top of the rocket, the charges ignite. It explodes in a brilliant shower of sparkling white light. Let's light a couple of them off." Sammy handed Chang one of the rockets and said, "Unwrap the fuse line and cut it to the length you want. You can also tie a short stick on the end near the fuse. It adds a little weight to help stabilize the rocket."

Chang left about a foot of fuse on the rocket. He used the remaining fuse to tie a stick to the end of the rocket. He leaned the rocket against a rock, pointed it upward and lit the fuse. Both men then retreated several feet to await the ignition. A little more than a minute later, the rocket lifted off with a whoosh. It arced skyward, left a trail of smoke and sparks, and headed out of sight. A few seconds later a blazing flash exploded overhead, followed by a series of smaller explosions and light bursts. The second rocket performed as well as the first, and soon several townspeople ran toward them shouting in panic that the gunpowder factory had blown up.

When Sammy explained to everyone that the explosions were only rockets, a few were disgruntled, but most chuckled and wanted him to launch another. Sammy went inside to get one more rocket, and sent it soaring into the sky amid cheers from the crowd. There were calls for more, but Sammy told them that would be all the displays for today. A collective groan of disappointment arose, but the miners were still laughing and talking about the rocket as they headed back to town.

After the crowd left, Sammy helped Chang load the packhorses with explosives and rockets. "What is your next step?" Sammy asked after they finished.

"The tong's horses are fine for working around here, but for a war with the Blackfoot I need one of their horses."

"We're a little short of appaloosas around here."

"Even if there were any they wouldn't be trained right. I need a horse trained by the Indians. I know how they react in emergencies. I do not know what these horses will do."

"How do you plan to get one?"

"The only way I know how, I will steal one," Chang grinned.

"I hope you don't get yourself shot in the process."

"So do I."

"I only wish I could go with you."

"You have more important things to do than being killed with me."

"Yeah, I guess I do at that," Sammy chortled.

The warming sun felt good on Chang's stiff hip, which had loosened considerably in the last hour. Although most American horses were trained for the rider to mount from the left side, Chang found that by leaping facedown onto the horse from the right side, he could swing his left leg over the horse while letting his right leg drop straight down. In that fashion he kept the movement in his right hip to a minimum and avoided the shooting pain in his leg. He mounted and dismounted several times until he could do it quickly and nearly painlessly. Chang felt fortunate the horse didn't seem to care from which side the man mounted. Sammy thought the whole scene humorous until Chang explained what he was doing and why.

At last, Chang was ready to proceed. The two men shook hands and Chang said, "Thank you Sammy, I do not think I could win this war without your help."

"You are welcome my friend."

Chang had learned his lesson about empty weapons after the Indians attacked him in town. Every firearm in his possession was fully loaded and within easy reach. Sammy handed Chang the guide ropes to the packhorses. Chang tied the guide ropes to the saddle and began his journey to the Blackfoot village.

As Chang rode, he massaged his right hip using techniques his mother taught him until the hip was nearly pain free. He walked the horse slowly. He was in no hurry to fight. Memories of Morning Bird and their wretched parting flooded his mind with guilt. He forced himself to think of happier times. He remembered her smile with one corner of her mouth curled slightly higher than the other. He saw her frown, her tears, and her enormous brown eyes as they gleamed in the light. He recalled every detail of her face as if she were standing before him. He saw her nose crinkle as she spoke, and he saw the tiny scar on her forehead she received as a child when she fell on a stone. He even saw the small mole on her left cheek. Then the mole moved, and Chang realized it was not a mole, but a slight movement in the underbrush ahead. He slipped the revolver from his jacket pocket almost unconsciously. Could this be the bandits? A cloud of dust tailed off over a rise. Horses? Moments later, several gunshots rang out in the distance, but Chang never saw their source. He kept plodding along, but didn't confront anyone—not, that is, until later that afternoon. A few miles later, he saw a rider following him on horseback, so distant he appeared to be nothing but a speck.

Chang was on edge. He heard no sound, no sign of any further ambush. Still the rider followed relentlessly. Must be an Indian, Chang thought, if the bandits were following they would have already attacked. The trail into the mountain started its climb a few miles later. Once he was amid the trees, he veered left off the path and concealed his horses in a thick grove. Chang surveyed the trail behind with the telescope, and quickly espied the rider. He was dressed in the traditional clothing of the Blackfoot and was riding an appaloosa. This is my chance to steal an Indian horse, Chang thought. He estimated the warrior was about an hour back. He concealed all signs of his tracks, and dug a hole to bury himself under the ground near the trail in the manner the Perce Nez had trained him. He did not want to take a chance that the warrior would spot him, so he concealed himself underground and waited motionless for the next hour. It was the first major test of his newfound skills.

At last, he heard hoof beats approach. When the horse passed next to him, he leapt from his place of concealment and threw himself over the horse, stripping the rider from its back. The startled horse ran a few dozen yards before it stopped to see what happened. Chang was about the strike the Indian, when he saw that the warrior was already unconscious. Chang was confused, until he saw a large splotch of blood on the right side of the Indian's torso. The Blackfoot had been shot. Maybe he met the bandits back there, Chang thought. That must have been what all the shooting was. Chang removed a bow and a quiver of arrows the Indian had strung over his shoulder and behind his back. He then took off the Indian's shirt and saw that although the bullet left a large hole in the warrior's side, it had not struck any organs.

Chang quickly gathered herbs nearby and patched the Indian warrior's side by Perce Nez healing methods. Chang knew the warrior needed additional care or he might not live. What was he to do? There were no real doctors in Bannack, just the barber who did a little surgery on the side. His most grievous patients nearly always died. The Perce Nez? This Blackfoot would never make it that far. No, his only option was the Blackfoot village. With luck, they might make it there by tomorrow. Chang cinched the makeshift bandage around the Indian's side as tightly as he could, tied the Indian to the appaloosa and headed toward the Blackfoot Village.

-ELEVEN-

CHANG PRESSED ONWARD until well after dark. When the horses began tripping over obstacles on the path he decided it was best to stop. Chang repacked the Blackfoot warrior's wound before leaving camp the next morning. The Indian awakened for the first time, and flinched when he saw his enemy, the Chinaman with the red headband, leaning over him. Chang used sign language to reassure the Indian and tell him he had nothing to fear. Chang gave his newfound ward a swallow of water, but afterward the Indian again lapsed into unconsciousness. Chang tied the young handsome bronzed man to his horse to ensure he didn't fall off. Chang threw the bow and quiver of arrows over his own shoulder behind his back, and set off. By the time the morning sun peaked over the mountaintop, camp was already an hour behind.

As they traveled, the warrior roused himself a few times and tried to speak to Chang, but the captain could not understand the Blackfoot language. When Chang tried to communicate by hand signs, the Indian would again pass out. Chang was ever alert for signs of danger, but was relieved to find no further complications during the trip, that is, at least, until they neared the Blackfoot village.

It was early afternoon when Chang recognized several landmarks that told him he was nearly to the village. Now what shall I do, he asked himself. If I proceed, someone is likely to shoot me, but I must make sure this warrior survives. I am tired of the wanton killings. I must put an end to this now, and I will do it at the Blackfoot village. Chang thought the best chance of living through the impending encounter was to stay close to the Blackfoot warrior. Maybe no one would dare try to shoot him if there were any chance of hitting the warrior.

Just outside the village, Chang heard the warning whistle of a hidden Blackfoot scout. Another whistle a little farther off answered. Chang pulled so close to the Indian warrior that their legs rubbed as they rode. What better shield could there be? Then all at once, the Blackfoot village came into view over the top of a hillock. Shouts from the village below stopped Captain Chang in his tracks. The men were arming themselves and preparing to attack. A warrior sprinted toward Chang while attempting to nock an arrow into the bowstring. Chang grabbed the wounded Indian's bow, nocked an arrow and let fly, neatly cutting the attacking Indian's bowstring. The Indian cried out in terror and fled.

Chang slapped the flanks of the wounded warrior's horse and sent it bounding into the village below. All the warriors Chang could see were running up the hill toward him on foot. He leapt from his horse, grabbed a bag of gunpowder bombs from one of the packs on a packhorse, lighted the fuse about a quarter inch from the wooden casing and tossed it down the hill. The resultant explosion sent Indians scattering. Chang tossed another for good measure, jumped on his horse and headed for the other side of the village. He lit fuses every several feet as he traveled until arriving at his destination.

From his new vantage point, Chang saw Indians running everywhere, and occasional explosions sounded. The captain undid the pack on the other packhorse and removed some of the rockets. He had meant to wait until the night of the full moon to light the rockets off and play on the Blackfoot superstitions, but it seemed to him that now was as good a time as any to finish this war one way or another. He lined up several rockets and pointed them toward the village. He kept the confusion rampant by lighting the rockets off one at a time, several seconds apart, and tossing a gunpowder bomb over the edge now and then.

When the bombs and ammunition were nearly expended, Chang mounted his horse. With a handgun in each jacket pocket, repeating rifle in one hand, sniper rifle across his knees and bow and arrows slung over his back he galloped down the hill to Chief Three Fingers' lodge. The chief stood in front of his lodge smiling at Chang as if welcoming home a prodigal son. Most tribal members were still running around camp obviously unaware that Chang had entered the village. Chief Three Fingers on the other hand, seemed to be expecting him. The captain was unsure of what was happening and dismounted the tong's horse cautiously. Chang asked in the Indian hand language, "What is happening?"

Chief Three Fingers looked surprised and replied, "I am happy to see you learned our hand language."

"I took lessons."

The chief smiled, "Thank you for saving my son."

"Your son?" Chang questioned. Then understanding dawned on him, "You mean the wounded warrior. He is your son?"

"Yes, my only son. He told me six armed white men who had faces covered with cloth attacked him. My son wounded two of the men before he escaped."

Just then, several warriors noticed Chang's presence in the camp. Many screamed their horrible war cries and charged forward. Chang raised the repeating rifle and whirled around. Chief Three Fingers placed himself between Chang and the warriors. The chief faced the warriors with his hands upraised. He shouted in the Blackfoot language that was still unintelligible to the captain. He pointed at his tent, held his side then lowered his arms. Gradually, the warriors lowered their weapons and began talking to each other. Most seemed much calmer, although a few of the women continued to shout to the warriors and point at Chang. Some of the warriors spoke to the women, who angrily returned to their lodges.

Chief Three Fingers turned back to Chang and said, "I told them you saved my son's life and that our war is now over. I told them that any warrior who continues the war will be banished from the tribe."

Chang said, "Thank you Chief Three Fingers. I am grateful, but who are the women who still seem so angry?"

"They are the widows of the warriors you killed. They will be angry, but all will be well, they will find new men and start new lives together. I am proud of you. I told my people once before that a war against you would be useless, that you would live on. You are an honorable adversary and still worthy to be called Yellow Chief."

"Thank you," said Chang, "You too are a fine man, and I am happy to call you my friend."

A voice called from inside Three Fingers' teepee. The Indian chief looked at Chang, pointed at the teepee entrance and nodded his head. Chang went inside where he found the wounded warrior lying on a buffalo skin. In broken English the warrior said, "You save life, me, you save me," and thumped his own chest with the tips of his fingers several times. Me thanks you."

"You are welcome my friend. I am also grateful to you. You will never know how grateful."

At first, the warrior looked puzzled, as if he didn't understand what Chang said. Then his face turned hard and he shouted something Chang did not understand. The wounded man pulled a knife from his waist and threw it. Chang fell back, certain that his end had come at last, but the knife was not meant for him. It pierced the hand of a woman. From her hand tumbled a tomahawk meant for the Chinese captain's head. Chang recognized the woman—the widow of Bent Gun who Chang had defeated in combat in this same village.

Chief Three Fingers grabbed the woman's arm and pulled the knife from the wound in her hand. Not a peep escaped her lips, but hatred seething in her eyes. Chang spoke to her in hand language and said, "I know of you anger, and I can only guess at how much the loss of you man means to you. I am sorry for all that has happened and I wish I could make it up to you. If there is anything I can do for you, anything to stop the hatred between us, I would do it."

The woman still glared at Chang, obviously not appeased. Chang took the knife from Chief Three Fingers and handed it to the woman. The Chinaman continued, "I offer you my scalp if it will bring peace between our people." He knelt before her and lowered his head. He expected excruciating pain to sear through the top of his head at any moment. A sob and cry of mourning from deep within the soul of the grief stricken woman pierced the camp. When Chang looked up, she lowered the knife to her side. Tentatively, Chang placed a hand upon the woman's shoulder and pulled her toward him. She threw her arms around the Chinese man as she shook with sorrow. Chang also erupted in tears and both wept uncontrollably. "I am so, so sorry," he said repeatedly. He knew that she didn't understand the words, but she would understood their meaning.

Chang led the woman outside. He unloaded one of the packhorses and gave the guide rope to her. He explained, "I want you to have this horse. I know it will not replace your man, but perhaps it can ease your burdens. I also promise to send you and your tribe supplies to help the women of all the warriors I have slain. I will do this every year for as long as you need them." The woman looked at the ground, nodded and led the horse away.

When Chang looked back at Chief Three Fingers, the old man smiled and said, "You will always be welcome here, but be careful on your way home today." Chang looked at him questioningly. "We still have scouts out who do not know yet that our war has ended." Chang took a deep breath and sighed slowly, as the old chief chuckled.

—　　—　　—

Chang was extra vigilant on his return to Bannack. It wouldn't be right to be killed by a Blackfoot warrior after the end of the war. Perhaps the warriors received word somehow, maybe by smoke signal, because he met no trouble on the way home—at least not from the Indians. He used the same camp he had the night before, and got an early start the following morning.

When Chang approached the clump of trees where the bandits attacked Chief Three Fingers' son, the captain heard a horse whinny. Above the trees floated a cloud of dust. Someone was awaiting him in ambush. Chang had an idea. He alit from the horse and gathered the few remaining fireworks and bombs from the packhorse. They worked on the Indians, he thought, so maybe they will work as well on the bandits. No sooner had he leaned the remaining rockets on a rock and pointed them toward the grove of trees when four riders galloped toward him, shouting and shooting. Each wore a bandana mask over his face. Chang calmly lit each of the fireworks, sending the bandits' terrorized horses bucking and running in circles. In spite of their disorganization, the bandits continued shooting in Chang's general direction.

Chang moved beside a small stream. He estimated the time he thought it would take the bandits to arrive at his location. He lit the bomb fuses and hid them under the water. He hoped that Sammy was right about them being waterproof. He galloped about a quarter of a mile away as if he were fleeing the bandits. When the bandits were nearly where the bombs were hidden, Chang stopped and whirled around to face the men. The bandits reined in their horses, and slowed to a trot, apparently thinking Chang had given up. One of the bandits shouted at Chang, telling him to drop his weapons. Chang spurred his horse to a walk toward the bandits. It was then the bombs exploded. All four bandits fell from their horses to the ground as the horses reared and fled. One man attempted to gather up his handgun from the ground. Chang fired his sniper rifle, knocking the gun out of reach. He hurried to reload, and when a second man tried to pick up a gun from the ground, Chang again shot the weapon away. The captain switched to his repeating rifle as he approached the four men. He didn't need the sniper rifle at this range.

When he got closer he ordered all the men to drop their gun belts. "You ain't gonna get away with this chink," said one of the bandits, who pulled a tin star from his shirt pocket. "I'm a lawman and these here are my deputies. We're arresting you for assaulting law enforcement officers." The men all started chattering, and laughing with each other. When Chang aimed his rifle at the forehead of the sheriff, all laughter ceased. The only sound was the breeze whipping the tree branches.

All four bandits eyed their weapons on the ground, and slowly inched toward them as their fingers slowly balled into fists and relaxed as they sized up their opponent. "I guarantee," threatened Chang, "that not one of you will live to see another sunrise if you go for those guns."

"Who to you think you're talking to chink?" said the sheriff. You can't do this to lawmen and get away with it. Every lawman in the territory will be gunning for you."

"Not all," shouted a voice. A man rode slowly from the trees.

"Marshal Fielding?" asked the Sheriff, "What are you doing here. Well, ain't no never mind about that. You're just in time to help me arrest this Chinaman. He is one of them bandits that's been working the area here. We was just trying to arrest him and he got the jump on us."

Chang tensed, unsure where the conversation was headed and if the marshal believed the sheriff's story or not. "Now Sheriff Plummer," chided the marshal, "you wouldn't be trying to mislead me now would you?"

"No sir marshal, so help me. We was just out here doing our duty."

"But that's just not quite the way I saw it," said the marshal. I've been tailing you since yesterday, but I suspected you for weeks. Now I finally caught you in the act. I hope you had a good time with the money and property you stole, because you aren't going to be able to spend any more of it."

"But marshal," protested Plummer, "you got things all wrong."

"No, you got things wrong months ago with your stealing and murdering."

"Marshal," the sheriff begged, "it just ain't right. You know how it is with law enforcement—people always taking potshots at you. The town just don't pay enough for that kind of risk."

"So quit and do something else."

"There ain't no money in nothing else around here neither."

"You took an oath sheriff, or maybe I should say ex-sheriff. You were in a position of trust. You are one of a very few people who could have made a difference in making this a better community. Instead, you let yourself slither on your belly, lower than the lowest blood sucking louse. You make more money than many good folks I know. Farmers put their lives, the lives of their families and all the property they own on the line for what they do. They suffer plagues of insects, droughts, late frosts and anything else the good Lord hands them. In any given year they could lose everything. Most years they don't make any more than you do, but you've got a guaranteed pay voucher which they don't. What's more, they don't hang out with a band of shiftless oafs like you chose to do. They put their backs and their bodies into everything they earn."

"Marshal, you can't put me in prison, I put many people behind bars there. They'd kill me."

"Now sheriff, you don't have to worry about that, I'll see to it personally."

"Really?" the sheriff sounded surprised.

"Sure, I'll even make it easy on you."

"What do you mean by that?"

"I'll make sure you never make it to prison. We'll hang you right here in Bannack. The territorial judge will be here tomorrow. We wouldn't want you to travel too far, it might be a tad uncomfortable in the back of the prison wagon. We ought to hang you seventeen times, once for each murder, but to make it extra easy on you we'll only hang you once. Yep, we'll make do with that. Hang you too many times your head will be likely to pop clean off. We wouldn't want that to happen, it makes too big a mess for the undertaker. Maybe I can even lengthen your lifespan a mite. If I can talk the executioner into tying your noose the wrong way, the rope won't snap your neck like it's supposed to. That'll give you another couple of minutes to repent of your wrongdoings while you kick around and slowly strangle to death. It would be no more than you deserve."

Sheriff Plummer's face was deathly pale. His hand went involuntarily to his throat, and he licked his lips. "Oh, by the way, did you know that a couple more of you men kicked the bucket yesterday. We took them to the barber for surgery, but they just didn't make it. They did confess to you being the ringleader. Seems like you've been losing quite a few men lately, now it's down to just you four. When we hang you," the marshal snapped his fingers, "it'll be like you never were. You won't be leaving any great gap in history, and it sure won't be any great loss to the town."

Chang gathered up the bandits' weapons and loaded them on the packhorse. He and the marshal rode herd on the gang, who walked and complained every step of the ten miles to Bannack. Once the brigands were locked in the town jail, Chang told the marshal, "I am mighty relieved to be rid of them. If I had to hear about one more complaint from Sheriff Plummer, I might have shot off his toe just to relieve him of his blister.

Marshal Fielding and Chang stepped outside where the marshal asked, "I might have some news for you in a bit. Where will you be staying so I can get in touch with you if I need to?"

Chang answered, "I'll be at the Chinese tong house."

"Great. Thanks for everything. You helped put an end to the thieving around here, at least for now. It'll likely start up again sooner or later. Just can't have this many people spending all their days looking for gold and never expect any problems. Hopefully, I'll see you later on this evening."

Chang was puzzled as Marshal Fielding walked away. He wondered what news the marshal might have for him. Chang shrugged and reached up to rub the top of his head. Something was missing. It was then he realized that he had taken off his identifying red headband. He felt almost naked without it. He pulled it from his pocket and placed it back on his head. Now it felt better.

Chang ended a war without anyone else killed and he stopped a gang of violent highwaymen. He ought to feel ecstatic, but he didn't. He remounted the horse and headed back toward the tong house. He stared at the ground dejectedly, not yet even fully aware of his despondency. As he dismounted his horse, a voice behind him said, "Howdy stranger."

Without turning to face the newcomer, Chang asked, "What are you doing here?"

The voice answered, "Isn't a wife supposed to greet her man after a hard day at work?"

Chang whirled around. Grabbing Morning Bird's arms, he fixed her eyes in his. "Do you mean that? Am I really your man?"

"Sure as shootin'," Morning Bird said in a western twang.

Chang took her in his arms and broke down. For someone who hadn't cried since he was a child, he was doing a lot of it lately. Equal parts of grief, passion and relief flooded over him. A quiet aching racked his mind for weeks, but now it was free. He shuddered uncontrollably in her arms. He knew he should feel abashed, but he didn't. He was home—home at last with the woman who would be his forever.

Chang composed himself, never realizing until this moment his capacity for depth of emotion. He gazed into Morning Bird's eye, "I love you," he told her, never having meant anything more in his life.

Morning Bird looked into his eyes, "Come to dinner," was all she said.

"Let me get washed up first," Chang told her. "I need to get the trail dust washed off."

"No, come now. You smell wonderful."

"I'm not sure the rest of your family will think so."

Morning Bird simply giggled, and led him by the arm toward her house. When they arrived, a horse was tied to the hitching post out front, but Chang was so giddy he barely noticed it. When they entered the house Zeb was there sitting in a chair. He stood and hugged Chang, saying, "Welcome home pardner. I heared you had yourself quite a time with them there Blackfoot."

"Indeed I did," said Chang, "but what are you doing here?"

"Oh, I had business in town and I thought I'd drop in to give my old pal Captain Chang a visit. Besides, this here's the best place in town for grub so let's eat. I'm starved."

Zeb kept the conversation focused on Chang's experiences with the Blackfoot and with the bandits. Chang hadn't intended to say much about either, but Zeb wasn't about to let him get away with changing the topic. Although Zeb kept asking for details, Chang had the idea that Zeb knew as much about what happened as Chang himself did. Zeb got up and looked out the window several times during the meal. The fifth time he peered out the window he said, "Looks like you got visitors." The sound of approaching horses' hooves soon filled the air.

Morning Bird's feet barely touched the floor as she flew to the door to open it before the visitors had a chance to knock. Her smile was intoxicating. The new guests smiled as broadly as she did. Soon everyone in the room was grinning in what nearly seemed a carnival atmosphere. Marshal Fielding was the first through the door, followed by several people Chang recognized as town bigwigs. The mayor was there, along with several town council members.

Zing Yong offered, "Please be seated everyone." There were barely enough chairs to seat everyone. In fact, the tong's son sat on the floor for lack of seating. "I think everyone here knows one another, right? Good. I think everyone knows why we gathered here, except Captain Chang of course, but he will find out soon enough." There were snickers all around. "Captain Chang, I must first give you some bad news. Not long ago I told you that the Chinese emperor began to nationalize the army. That nationalization is now fully gripping the nation. General Zeng Gudfan could have chosen to save himself—instead he remained to help evacuate many people slated for execution. General Gudfan sacrificed himself for those he served. He was removed from office and executed several weeks ago."

"How could this be?" protested Chang, "You only told me of the nationalization a few days ago."

"Another of our ships entered port yesterday with updated news from China."

"But why General Gudfan? He was a good man who saved my life. I would not be here today if not for him."

The tong answered, "It is the life he chose. He lost his life in the service of others. He saved many lives. He sent a shipload of prominent people to America. If they had not come they most definitely would have been executed. Their lives, as yours, will continue. Nevertheless, although the general is dead, he will live on. The good general's life will continue forward through the lives of those he saved and through the lives of their children, including the children of Captain Chang and Morning Bird." Chang felt Morning Bird tense in embarrassment. "Through the sacrifice of General Gudfan, through his endeavors, your life and the lives of your children are made possible. Make your life worthwhile. Teach your children so the sacrifice of General Gudfan will have meaning and importance."

Chang looked at Morning Bird, then back at the tong and said, "I will Tong Zing Yong, I promise."

Zing Yong then said, "I thought you might like to meet a couple saved by General Gudfan. He pointed toward a doorway, and in walked a handsome Chinese couple, Chang's mother and father. Chang jumped from his chair, bowed politely to his parents, and hugged them both as they all wept openly for joy. After several minutes, Chang led his parents into the room and offered his seat to his mother. Then the tong said, "We are all grateful your parents are here, but we have more news for you."

"Nothing could be better than what I have already received today."

"Nevertheless, you may be pleased to hear this too. Mr. Mayor, the floor is yours."

In a typical politician's blustery voice the mayor said, "Yes, well, uh, thank you Honorable Tong Zing Yong. I would like to announce that there is a position open in the town if you are interested."

"A position?" Chang asked, "What kind of position?"

"Well, uh, yes, um," stammered the mayor, "I understand that you will soon be out of a job in your military. It, uh, also seems that with the arrest of the sheriff the position has become available. We would be deeply honored if you would accept the job. Marshal Fielding recommends you highly. Unfortunately, the job doesn't pay much, but if you are ever short of cash, there are several odd jobs around town where you could earn extra money, including, er, uh, my hardware store if you are interested." There was a small murmur of voices, and the mayor looked around warily. "But, er, uh, of course your law enforcement position would have priority over any, er, uh, other enterprises you might wish to consider."

"I appreciate the officer sir," protested Chang, "but I am not an American citizen."

"That could be a problem," answered the mayor, "but, er, Zeb here says he has connections in Washington, some pretty high connection, if you take my meaning."

"President Lincoln?" Chang asked, looking at Zeb, who simply nodded.

"At any rate, er, uh," continued the mayor, "Zeb seems to think he can get the citizenship papers for you and your parents rushed through a little faster than usual. So what do you say, would you become our new sheriff?

Chang looked at Morning Bird for confirmation. She smiled and nodded. "It would be an honor sir," he told the mayor, to the cheers of everyone in the room.